L-4 ≤In-1 0

W9-DIA-454

No Contact

Sandra Diersch

James Lorimer & Company Ltd., Publishers
Toronto

James Lorimer & Company Ltd. acknowledges the support of the Ontario Arts Council. We acknowledge the support of the Government of Canada through the Book Publishing Industry Development Program (BPIDP) for our publishing activities. We acknowledge the support of the Canada Council for the Arts for our publishing program. We acknowledge the support of the Government of Ontario through the Ontario Media Development Corporation's Ontario Book Initiative.

Cover illustration: Greg Ruhl

Library and Archives Canada Cataloguing in Publication

Diersch, Sandra
    No contact / Sandra Diersch.

(Sports stories)
ISBN 978-1-55277-025-2 (bound). ISBN 978-1-55277-024-5 (pbk.)

    I. Title. II. Series: Sports stories (Toronto, Ont.)

PS8557.I385N6 2008   jC813'.54   C2008-904679-X

James Lorimer & Co. Ltd.,	Distributed in the United States by:
Publishers	Orca Book Publishers
317 Adelaide Street West,	P.O. Box 468
Suite 1002	Custer, WA USA
Toronto, Ontario	98240-0468
M5V 1P9	
www.lorimer.ca	

Printed and bound in Canada.

CONTENTS

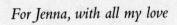

For Jenna, with all my love

Special thanks to:
Joe for answering my many questions about hockey and "tweaking" my hockey scenes, the Ridge Meadows' PeeWee B Barracudas ice hockey team for letting me hang out and get to know them, Renee and her Pathfinders for allowing me to attend their meetings, Joan for sharing her knowledge about older child adoption, Josh for sharing his knowledge of hockey, Rose who helped with the yoga poses, and finally, Ellen for her invaluable suggestions, comments and advice.

1 Forever Family

Debbie Lowell rolled back and forth across the driveway on her in-line skates, stick-handling the orange plastic puck. She tapped it with the front, then the back, of her beat-up hockey stick, wondering how she should go for a goal. Greg stood in net, watching her. He had stopped five of her last seven shots. For an old guy that was pretty good. For Debbie, a right wing on the Maple Ridge Lightning girls' ice hockey team, that was not so good.

"Well?" he asked. "You going to shoot any time soon? I'm cold."

In answer, Debbie fired a shot. She caught Greg off guard — the puck slid past him and came to rest in the dirty netting. She lifted her arms above her head in celebration. Greg fished out the puck and shot it back to her.

"Good one," he said.

"Thank you. I thought so."

She skated around a couple of times, keeping the puck just in front of her rolling feet, then shot from the left side. Greg stopped it and passed it back to her. Again and again Debbie shot — backhand, forehand, from the left, from the right, until her arms felt like jelly and her nose was running from the cold. It missed the net more often than it hit, though, and Debbie felt the familiar anger starting to rise.

"Aw, just go in!" she hollered when yet another shot went wide. She banged her stick on the wet pavement.

"Hey," Greg said. "Relax. That's why we're practicing, right?"

"Do you have to be so darn positive all the time?" Debbie snapped.

Greg went to fish the puck out from beneath the neighbour's car. "Besides, it's not all about scoring the goals."

"Whatever! It's all about scoring the goals." Debbie caught sight of Greg's raised eyebrows and stopped. "Well, it's mostly about scoring," she muttered.

Greg passed her the puck. "Watch the attitude, please, Deb," he said mildly. "Or I'll start with my clichés."

"Oh, please, not the clichés," Debbie cried, skating around in circles with the puck. "Anything but the clichés!"

In the year since Greg and Angie Lowell had

adopted her, Debbie had learned to deal with her new dad's sense of humour and teasing — well, mostly. It was one of the things she loved — and hated — about him.

She turned to skate backward, concentrating hard on what she was doing so she wouldn't land on her butt. It was definitely easier to skate backward on wheels than on the narrow metal blades of her hockey skates. And it was easier staying upright on the road than it was on ice. Debbie glanced around with satisfaction. Although Maple Ridge, BC, had its fair share of hills, the Lowells' neighbourhood was flat, and living on a small cul-de-sac meant they could play road hockey safely.

Across the street a garage door rattled and Debbie looked up to see her best friend, Paige Arnold. Paige waved when she saw Debbie, a grin appearing on her freckled face.

"Wanna play?" Debbie called out.

"Sure! Just let me get a stick and some gloves." Paige disappeared back into the garage.

"Do you mind, Dad?" Debbie asked.

Greg shook his head. "The more the merrier."

Debbie pretended to gag at the cliché.

"Aren't you guys frozen yet?" Angie asked, appearing suddenly on the front step, a jacket thrown around her shoulders. A blur of red and white fur rushed past her and leaped at Debbie, stub tail wagging.

11

"It's better if you keep moving," Debbie said, rubbing the dog's head with her mittened hand. Debbie thought having Poker as a pet was one of the best things about being adopted by the Lowells.

"Yes, I bet it is. Well, when you're ready to come in, I'll have hot chocolate ready."

"Why don't you come out and play with us?" Greg suggested. "Paige is coming over. We could have teams."

Angie shivered. "No, thanks. It's a little too brisk for me."

"That's a good excuse," Debbie said with a cheeky grin.

"What's that supposed to mean? Are you saying I'm lazy?"

"Hey, you're the one who said it. Not me."

"In your mother's defence —" Greg began.

"There is no defence! Mom likes us to come out and exercise. Then, when we get cold, she joins us for hot chocolate in front of the fire!"

"Well, not in the summer," Angie said. As the laughter faded, Angie turned to go back in the house.

Greg caught Debbie's eye and raised one eyebrow, nodding his head in Angie's direction. Debbie bugged out her eyes at him and shook her head, but he looked right back at her, until finally, Debbie gave in.

"Mom?" she called, stopping Angie as she was about to shut the door. "We really could use another person."

For a split second Angie and Greg exchanged looks. Then Angie nodded. "Just let me get something else on."

Paige arrived, carrying a stick that was way too big for her, and wearing an old Canucks hat over her red curls.

"That stick is awfully big," Debbie observed. "Doesn't your brother have anything smaller?"

Paige shook her head. "He wasn't into hockey, just basketball. I'll make it work. It's not like this is the Grey Cup or anything."

Debbie laughed. "In hockey it's the Stanley Cup," she explained. "The Grey Cup is for football." She bent down to undo her skates and change into her sneakers. Greg had told her it wasn't fair for her to be on blades when the rest of them were in shoes.

"Whatever," Paige said with an easy shrug. "Hey, Deb, did you hear what happened on Friday?" Paige lowered her head, keeping one eye on Greg. "Ethan Cho asked Claudine to go to the movies with him! And she said yes!"

"Why'd she do that?"

Paige pushed Debbie playfully with her gloved hands. "What do you mean, why'd she do that? Claudine likes Ethan, that's why."

Claudine wasn't the first girl in their grade seven class to go on a date, but Debbie didn't have time, between hockey, basketball and Pathfinders, to go on dates. And, although there were a couple of guys in her class who she thought were kind of cool, there wasn't one she would want to go on a date with.

"I wish Carter would ask me to go to the movies with him," Paige continued, her voice suddenly dreamy.

Deb couldn't believe her ears. "Carter? Carter Dixon? The only things Carter is interested in are his video games, Paige."

Paige sighed. "Yeah, I know. Oh, well."

Angie joined them on the driveway five minutes later, carrying a hockey stick and looking determined. "Okay, what do I have to do?" she asked, gripping the stick tightly.

Debbie bit back a smile as she repositioned her mom's hands on the shaft of the stick and showed her how to control the puck. Angie looked so awkward and ill at ease that Debbie began to regret inviting her to join them.

"What are the teams?" Paige asked.

"You and I can be a team, Paige," Greg said before Debbie could answer.

"I guess that means you and me, Deb," Angie said.

Debbie forced a smile. Maybe it would start to rain again, or maybe lightning would strike.

Debbie dropped the puck, and ran away with it. She circled the net, then passed the puck to her mom. Angie trapped the puck and passed it back to Debbie, but Paige intercepted it and passed to Greg. Greg headed for the net. Angie stood still, watching him.

"Go get him, Mom! He's going to score!" Deb shouted as the puck went in the back of the goal. Greg and Paige raised their arms in celebration. Paige even made crowd noises.

Debbie let out a long breath. "You want to try to stay between those guys and the net," she explained to Angie. "We're trying to prevent them from scoring."

Angie nodded and they started again. Debbie won the face-off and passed the puck to her mom. Angie missed the pass, but ran after the puck and gained control of it. She ran toward the goal, Greg right at her heels. Laughing, Angie went right then left. Finally, Greg poked the puck away from her with an evil laugh.

"Hey!" she cried and stopped running.

Debbie chased after her dad, who passed to Paige, waiting near the net. She shot it in. Debbie stopped running. She leaned on her knees, breathing hard.

"Why'd you stop running?" Debbie asked Angie. "You have to stay with the play, Mom. You can't just stop."

"Sorry, I was out of breath."

Debbie opened her mouth, then closed it again. She should never have agreed to this in the first place. Her mom was useless when it came to sports. Completely useless.

★ ★ ★

A half hour later, noses and cheeks scarlet, the Lowell family collected in the living room. Paige had gone home, loudly chanting, "We are the champions!" Angie drew the drapes and turned on the lamps. The fire was lit and Poker lay in front of it, panting gently from the heat. Debbie accepted the mug of steaming hot chocolate topped with marshmallows from her mom, then curled up in her favourite chair. Greg stretched out next to Poker and rested his head on the dog's side.

"When's dinner ready?" Debbie asked.

"About an hour," Angie said, handing Greg his drink.

"Can I have something to eat?"

"Sure. Why don't you get us all crackers and some of Gran's antipasto?"

Debbie came back a few minutes later with a plate. "I got some of that yummy cheese too," she said, setting the plate on the coffee table.

"Did you bring some napkins?" her mom asked.

Debbie returned with a handful of napkins, dropping them beside the plate. She helped herself to a cracker spread thick with antipasto. She closed her eyes and chewed dramatically.

"This is so-o-o good," the words leaking out from around a mouthful of cracker crumbs and zesty vegetables.

"For heaven's sake, Deb," Angie cried, "finish what's in your mouth before you speak! And use a napkin. I don't want crumbs all over the rug."

Debbie swallowed and wiped her mouth with a napkin. "There. Happy?"

"Hey, Ange," Greg broke in before Angie could reply. "Have you got a date for your concert?"

Angie nodded. "We have. A Tuesday evening mid-March. That small wind ensemble from Port Coquitlam has agreed to come, so it should be a very pleasant evening."

"Looking forward to it, right, Deb?"

"Is it going to be the same stuff you've been practicing?" asked Debbie, frowning. "'Cause it's not really my style."

"That 'stuff' is a very old, very famous concerto, Deb," her mom told her.

"Sor-ry."

"Play a bit for us, Ange," Greg said, with a warning glance at Debbie.

Debbie rolled her eyes but said nothing. It was bad enough hearing that old boring music when she was locked in her room. Why couldn't her mom play stuff that was a bit more now? What was with the fascination with old dead guys?

Debbie wondered, not for the first time, what kinds of things her birth mother liked, if she was into classical music or more modern stuff. Maybe her birth mother was a jock, like Debbie. Debbie felt an old, familiar twinge in her chest and cleared her throat. She hadn't felt it much this past year, but every once in a while it returned. Would there come a time when it didn't?

Angie and Greg encouraged her to talk about her birth mother with them. They even wanted her to talk about her foster parents, Darlene and Steve, if she wanted. And sometimes Debbie did talk about her old life. But this new life was so full and different. There just wasn't much time to think about the loneliness and sadness of that other life.

Poker stood up and shook. Debbie blinked and brought herself back into the cozy living room. Angie was at the piano, arranging her music and the lighting. When she began the piece, Debbie noticed her dad closing his eyes. *Does closing your eyes help make it more bearable?* she wondered.

The music filled the living room with waves of sound. Sometimes Angie's music crashed and pounded on the shore and other times, it lapped gently. Debbie's eyes closed and she was swept up and carried along on the journey.

Greg's sudden enthusiastic clapping and whistle alerted Debbie that Angie had finished playing. Her eyes snapped open and she snuck a quick look at Greg, wondering if he'd seen her closed eyes. Had he noticed her enjoying the music?

"Well," Angie asked, "what did you think?"

"You play a lot better than the students who come,

that's for sure," Debbie admitted.

Angie shook her head but was laughing as she said, "I'll take that as praise. And I should play better than my students, I've been playing a lot longer. They'll get better with practice. Same as with scoring goals, right?"

Debbie smiled. "Never lose a teaching moment, do you?" she said, reaching for another piece of cheese.

"Your mother could have been a concert pianist, Deb," Greg announced, sitting up. "She was headed for the stage when I met her and ruined her career."

"Greg Lowell, stop it. Don't listen to him, Deb. I'm afraid I was never good enough to have that kind of career. Just good enough to teach and make music for myself and my family."

"Well, it was good. I could never play like that."

"You could if you learned. Come see," Angie invited, patting the bench beside her.

"Naw."

"It's not that difficult — no more so than learning how to skate and play hockey."

"She even taught me a bit, Deb, believe it or not," Greg said.

"No, thanks." Debbie shook her head.

"Okay," Angie said, standing up. "I guess I'll go see about that roast, shall I?"

2 On the Ice

Debbie clenched her fingers around an imaginary hockey stick, her wrists flicking left and right in time with the windshield wipers, her shoulders leaning in.

In her head, the voice spoke low and steady, "Keep your head up, eyes on the puck, follow the play, keep your concentration. Stick on the ice, shoulders loose, skate smooth …"

Angie's light chuckle brought Debbie out of herself and back into the warm car. "What?"

"Just enjoying your pre-game ritual," Angie told her. "There are team psychologists who could use you as an example of how to use visualization."

"What's that supposed to mean?"

"I'm not making fun of you, Deb," her mom assured her. "Teams of all kinds, not just hockey, hire sport psychologists to work with players on visualization. Visualization is when you picture yourself in a situation, for example, tonight's game. You are visualizing skating down the ice, controlling the puck, watching for teammates." Angie paused for a moment. "I do it myself before I perform. I imagine my hands above the keyboard, picture the notes on the page, hear the music in my head."

Debbie hadn't known what the hockey practicing inside her head was called, but she did it a lot. Sometimes, when her school work was just too confusing, when the numbers in her math text wouldn't cooperate or the answers to social studies questions wouldn't come to her, she'd imagine she was geared up and on the ice, scoring goal after goal. She was glad there was a word for it. Now, if Mr. Joseph or the resource teacher bothered her about daydreaming, she could tell them she was visualizing.

"It's important to be mentally ready when you're going to perform," Angie continued. "Whether it's playing hockey or playing the piano. It helps you play better."

Debbie closed her eyes and took a breath, gathering her thoughts again. But her mom kept talking. Debbie frowned and tried to block out the sound.

"What do you think, Deb? Deb?" Angie's raised voice broke through Debbie's concentration.

"What?"

"You don't need to be rude," her mom told her. "I was just asking a question."

"I'm trying to prepare for the game, Mom," Debbie

explained. "But you keep interrupting me. You just finished saying mental preparation was important."

Angie's face went red. She cleared her throat. "You're right, I did. I'm sorry I interrupted you."

Debbie turned back to the window. A few minutes later, the car pulled into the arena parking lot. Debbie's pulse quickened. She loved playing hockey, but it was a little intimidating playing in front of friends and family. She'd only been playing for four months and there were still times when she landed on her rear, or swung her stick to have it hit nothing but air.

"Is Dad coming to watch?" she asked.

"He'll be here as soon as he's done with his staff meeting. We'll sit in our usual seats."

Debbie hoisted her bag out of the trunk and set it down on the pavement. *Thank goodness for the wheels*, she thought as she picked up the handle, *because my equipment bag weighs a ton!*

"Got everything?"

"Yeah. You don't have to ask every time, you know," Deb complained. "I'll see you later."

Angie pulled Debbie into a one-armed hug and kissed the top of her head. Debbie jerked away. With a last backward wave, she made her way inside the building. Just walking through the doors made the blood pump harder through her veins and her senses tingle. Voices echoed off the cement floors and walls, the cold air brushed her skin, the smell of old sweat and leather filled her nostrils. She could taste the ice.

"Hey, Deb," Amelia Larsen said, nudging Debbie with her stuffed bag.

"Oh, hi, Amelia."

"Are you totally psyched for this game?" Amelia picked up her own pace to stay with Debbie. "'Cause I am. They beat us pretty bad last time, but Mom says we're better prepared for them this time." Amelia's mother was the coach of their team, the Lightning.

Debbie pulled open the heavy door and Amelia's voice was immediately lost in the excited babble of the dressing room. Girls in various stages of suiting up stood or sat around the room. As usual, the smell of stale sweat mixed with the slightly sweet scent of hair products. Debbie grinned as she made her way inside and searched for a spot on the bench. Shoving aside a roll of tape and a helmet, she dropped down beside Amelia.

"What is that smell? Is that your socks, Hannah?" Meghan, the team captain, asked, wrinkling her nose.

"Shut up! They're clean." Hannah shot Meghan a dirty look.

"Gotta put soap in the water, Hannah," someone else called from across the room.

Debbie joined in the laughter as she hunted in her bag for her shin pads and socks. Finding them, she began the long, involved process of suiting up.

"So, Mom says the whole team has been working

real hard lately. She figures we'll do better against the Blades tonight," Amelia said.

"That'd be nice," Debbie muttered, thinking of the smoke show last time they'd played the Blades. The Lightning had lost 6–0.

"You've been working hard, Debbie," Amelia said, her blond head bent over her open bag. "I overheard my mom telling somebody how impressed she was with you."

Amelia kept talking but Debbie didn't hear anything further. She couldn't pretend that she wasn't happy to hear her teammate's words. Amelia's mom, Coach Steph Larsen, didn't hand out praise unless it was earned. Debbie stood up to pull on her pants, pulling the laces tight and secure around her waist, and then grabbed her dark blue jersey.

"Did she say anything else about me?" Debbie asked Amelia, her voice muffled by the heavy fabric of her jersey. She pulled her head through and adjusted the shoulders.

"Not really. Just that you picked up the sport pretty easily."

"Really?" Debbie ached to ask more questions, but Amelia turned to speak to someone else. Disappointed, Debbie sat down and pulled on her silver hockey skates. She began lacing them, grunting as she worked to get them tight enough.

"Everyone good in there?" a voice called from the

other side of the dressing-room door.

"Yes!" the girls chorused.

The door banged open and Coach Steph came through the door, followed by her assistants, Coach Mitch and Coach Nancy.

"All right, listen up, players!" Coach Steph said, resting one foot on the bench near Debbie. "Last time we played this team, it didn't go too well."

"As if we need reminding," Hannah muttered.

Debbie swallowed a grin and reached into her bag for her gloves. She followed every word her coach said as she zipped her bag shut and slipped the gloves on. Her stomach was jumpy and her mouth had gone dry.

"All you girls are playing well, reading each other. Let's keep it up and get these guys." Coach Steph paused and looked around the room, meeting the eyes of each of her players. "Play good, solid defence. When we're in their end, be the first to the puck. Use crisp hard passes. But most of all, remember to —"

"HAVE FUN!" they all shouted, finishing her sentence.

Coach nodded one last time. She held the door open as, one by one, led by their goalie, Kira, the Lightning made their way out to the ice for warm-up.

"Keep up the good work tonight, Deb," Coach Steph said as Debbie passed.

Her coach's words rang in Debbie's head, echoing what Amelia had told her. Debbie hadn't paid much attention to Amelia before, but maybe she should take the time to get to know her.

★ ★ ★

Debbie leaned forward against the battered boards, her eyes following the puck as it slid across the ice from player to player. Sticks banged the ice as three players fought for possession in front of the Lightning bench.

"Get in there hard, Meghan!" Coach Steph called. "You too, Charlie! Fight for it!"

"Come on, Lightning!" Debbie shouted.

At last, Meghan got possession of the puck. Keeping watch for an open wing, she skated hard toward centre ice, crossed the line, and delivered a cross-ice pass to Vanessa. The puck slid wide of Vanessa's stick, so she hustled after it, just ahead of the Blades defence. Debbie clutched her own stick hard, her whole body moving with Vanessa's as she skated for the Blades net. Two defence loomed in front of her, digging for the puck. Vanessa passed off to Meghan. The pass was picked off and the puck shot down the ice. Quickly, the Blades made a complete line change.

"Amelia's line on the gate. Keep your feet moving!" Coach Steph called, banging her clipboard against the boards.

Meghan and the rest of her line skated up to the bench as fresh players completed the line change. Adrenaline pumped through Debbie as she hurried toward the puck. Play had moved over centre ice. A

Blades forward moved in on Kira. Debbie caught up to the puck, fighting for possession. She wobbled and almost lost her balance, but managed to stay on her feet. The Blades player gained body position on Debbie. Debbie struggled to move around her, her breath coming out in hard bursts. She poke-checked the puck neatly away from the Blades forward. Amelia scooped it and raced back up the ice, eyes open for a passing lane to one of her linemates.

"Way to go, girls!" Coach Steph cried as the parents cheered.

Debbie skated faster, feeling a new burst of energy. She skated to the right of the goalie and set up an attack triangle. Amelia skated around behind the net and stopped.

"Amelia!" Debbie called. Amelia's pass around the net hit Deb's stick with a satisfying slap.

"Take the shot, Deb!" Coach Steph screamed.

Debbie wound up and took a low, hard snap shot at the goal. The puck hit the Blades goalie in the pads and rolled back out. Amelia and the Blades defender fought for it, but Amelia won out. She shot again.

The puck disappeared beneath the goalie's equipment. The goalie squeezed herself against the ice, but the puck rolled loose. Amelia pounced on it and slapped it into the net behind the bewildered goaltender.

Screams erupted as the puck crossed the line into the net.

Amelia and the rest of Debbie's line congratulated each other with smacks on the helmet and back, while the crowd stomped and cheered from the stands. The girls skated past the bench for a fly-by, slapping their teammates' hands, exhausted but thrilled.

"That was a good, solid effort, girls," Coach Steph told them with a huge grin. "Let's keep up the momentum out there! Keep your feet moving! Active sticks!"

Debbie squirted water into her mouth, then looked behind her to where Coach Steph stood, eyes on the play. She glanced down, caught Debbie's eye and smiled.

"Good shift, Deb. Way to go."

Debbie muttered, "Thanks," and ducked her head. She itched to get back on the ice. Maybe next time she'd get the goal. And maybe Coach Steph would be even happier with her.

3 Pathfinding

"Since you've decided we're camping in a couple of weeks, you need to start organizing it." Diana, the leader of Debbie's Pathfinder unit, handed out paper and pens to the girls gathered around the table. "Tonight we're going to start planning our menus. And no, Kelsie, we are not eating mac and cheese for dinner every night," she said, looking directly at the girl sitting beside Debbie.

Debbie smirked and Kelsie shot her a dirty look. "You'd eat KD every night too, if you could. So what are you laughing at?"

"I'm never allowed to eat KD. My mom insists on making mac and cheese from scratch," Debbie said, sticking her legs out in front of her.

"But your mom's mac and cheese is so good!" Paige cried. "I wish my mom cooked as good as Angie."

"Can we get on with this?" one of the older girls

demanded. "So, what are we going to eat for break-fast?"

"Pancakes?" Debbie suggested. "With maple syrup and blueberries." Her mouth watered just thinking about her mom's blueberry pancakes.

Kelsie wrote *Pancakes* on the sheet of paper. "Well, I'm good with just plain cereal," she said. The other girls loudly shouted her down.

"Come on, Kels!" Paige said when the noise subsided. "You gotta have something more exciting than cereal at camp."

"Hot dogs?"

Debbie screwed up her face. "How can you eat those things? Don't you know what they're made of? Why don't we do chili, or spaghetti and meatballs?"

"Not everyone has an amazing cook for a mother like you do, Deb," Paige reminded her. "Besides, hot dogs cooked over a fire are the best."

Debbie raised her eyebrows, unconvinced, while Kelsie added *Hot dogs* to the list.

As they worked, Debbie glanced down at her clothing every once in a while and smiled to herself. She'd longed to join Guides when she was a foster kid, and now here she was, a Pathfinder, complete with a uniform and camping trips. The other girls in her unit were pretty cool too. And, although Debbie had some-times had trouble getting along with adults in charge, their two leaders, Mizuki and Diana, were okay.

"Okay," Kelsie said, pulling Debbie back to the present. "We've got two more meals to do."

"And snacks! Don't forget snacks," Paige reminded everyone. "Especially s'mores."

"What are s'mores?"

Paige and Kelsie stared at Debbie and gasped in disbelief. "You've never had s'mores? Oh, Deb, you really are deprived." Kelsie patted Debbie's shoulder, shaking her head sorrowfully. "First you roast a marshmallow over a campfire."

"Then you get a piece of chocolate," Paige broke in.

"A big piece of chocolate." Kelsie indicated the size with her hands, nodding.

"Right," continued Paige. "You put a big piece of chocolate on a graham cracker. Then you put the toasted marshmallow on the chocolate and put another graham cracker on top to make a sandwich."

"Then you eat it."

Kelsie and Paige moaned in unison, falling back in their chairs. Debbie just stared at them, a sneer turning up the corners of her mouth. Amelia looked doubtful too.

"You have no idea, Deb," Kelsie said. "No idea." She wrote the word SNACKS in big letters at the bottom of the page.

"I just thought of another one!" Paige cried out. "Banana boats!"

Paige and Kelsie looked at each other and began their whole act all over again.

Near the end of the meeting, while the rest of the girls were arguing about how much milk they'd need for the weekend, Paige leaned over to Debbie and tugged on her sleeve.

"We need someone else in our tent," she whispered. "What about Kelsie?"

Debbie glanced at Kelsie, then over at Amelia. "I was thinking we should ask Amelia," she said.

"Amelia?"

"What's wrong with Amelia?"

"Nothing! I just don't know her that well and …"

"Well, this'll be a good way to get to know her," Debbie said. "We'll ask her after the meeting."

When the meeting ended a half hour later, Debbie caught Paige's eye. Grabbing their coats, they hurried after Amelia.

"Hey, Amelia," Debbie called, pulling on her coat as she ran. "Wait up. Paige and I wanted to ask you if you want to be in our tent."

Amelia looked in surprise from one girl to the other. "Me? Are you sure?"

"Absolutely!" Debbie said, elbowing Paige.

"Yeah, it'll be fun," Paige said obediently.

"I guess. Sure, thanks! We'll have so much fun! I'm going to bring some playing cards — I know the greatest card games — and we can talk all night."

Amelia, Paige, and Debbie walked out of the community centre together into the cold January evening. Their breath curled before them as they headed for the parking lot.

Angie was standing outside the Larsen's van, chatting with Coach Steph. She looked up and smiled as the girls approached. "Hey, how was your meeting?" she asked.

"Fine."

Amelia pulled open the sliding rear door of the van and climbed in. She stepped over several empty food wrappers and an abandoned water bottle, then had to move a pile of papers before she could sit down. Debbie watched, her thoughts going to Angie's car. Most of the time you could see the vacuum marks in the floor mats. And no one was allowed to eat in the car. If Poker went with them, he rode in a crate in the very back to contain his hair and dirt.

"Let me know what you want me to do, Steph," Debbie's mom said. "See you Thursday."

"Bye, Deb! Bye, Paige!" Amelia called from inside the van before her mom pulled away from the curb.

★ ★ ★

Debbie headed straight for the kitchen when she and her mom got in the house. Her stomach had been grumbling all the way home.

"Anything to eat?" Debbie asked, rummaging through the fridge.

"There's some of that vanilla yogurt you like," Angie suggested. "Did you talk about camp today?"

"Yeah, we planned the menus." Debbie spooned a generous helping of yogurt right from the family-sized container into her mouth.

"Please put it in a bowl, Deb," her mom chided.

Debbie found a bowl, poured a large serving, and sat at the table.

"I always loved going to camp," Angie continued. "I remember the first time I went to Camp Olave. I was eight or nine. I remember the little brown camp hats we wore. It was a big thrill to pin badges and shrink art to my hat. I probably still have it somewhere."

Angie poured herself some milk, then sat next to Debbie at the table. "We would sit around the campfire and sing songs and tell stories and do skits. It was great." She smiled, squeezing Debbie's shoulder. "I'm so excited for you, Deb. I know this is something you've been wanting to try."

"I've got some homework," Debbie said, sliding out from under Angie's warm hand. "Good night."

4 Differences

"Let's get a move on, girls!" Coach Steph yelled through the dressing-room door.

Debbie quickly pulled on her gloves and grabbed her stick. Out on the ice, she skated slowly, feeling the stretch in her hamstrings and quads. She picked up a puck and stick-handled it down the ice, picking up speed as she headed toward the net. The open goal yawned in front of her, and she sent the puck straight in, top shelf.

"Easy to score when the net's empty," Hannah teased, skating past.

Debbie picked up another puck and turned to skate backward, facing Hannah. Of all the things she'd had to learn about hockey, skating backward was one of the toughest. She always felt like she was about to topple over. She could never play defence! Hannah made it look so easy. Debbie passed the puck to her teammate, caught an edge, and landed heavily on her backside.

"Ouch!"

Coach Steph's words sang in her head as she got awkwardly to her feet, "Skating backward is like sitting in a chair — back straight, knees bent."

I should have stuck with basketball, Debbie thought. Basketball came so easily — always had. No bulky gear to work around, no slippery ice or awkward footwear. Just a pair of shorts, a shirt, some good high tops, and a ball — and go.

Debbie loved the squeak of the rubber-soled sneakers on the well-polished floor, the thud-thud-thud of the ball as it was dribbled from end to end of the court, and the calls of her teammates as they passed to each other. It was all good — the roughness of the ball under her fingers and the smell of rubber, the rush of speed as she tore up court, how the ball found her fingers effortlessly as she dribbled.

Debbie grinned to herself and slapped another puck at the empty net. Still, there was something about hockey. And she'd never had a coach like Coach Steph before. From what Debbie could see, Coach Steph knew everything about the game.

The coach blew her whistle and the entire team began skating hard around the rink. She blew the whistle again, two short blasts this time, and they all spun around and skated backward until the whistle went again. Over and over they went, until Debbie's lungs hurt and her muscles burned, and she thought she'd fall right over and never get up.

The whistle blew to end the drill, and the girls headed to the bench for a water break as Coach explained the next one. This time the team divided into two groups and went to opposite corners. On the whistle, one girl from each side skated in, circled centre ice, received a pass from one of the coaches, drove hard to the net, and shot.

Debbie stayed at the back of her line. It gave her time to watch the drill, to practice in her head before she actually had to do it. At her turn, she skated out, circled at centre, caught the pass (which in itself was pretty amazing), and drove for the net. But her shot went wide. She tensed, the muscles in her jaw tight with frustration.

"Good effort, Deb," Coach called out with a nod. She skated over. "Move your hands shoulder-width apart and really aim at your target! If the puck didn't hit the net, it's because you weren't aiming there! Got it?" Deb nodded. "And take your time before you shoot. Make sure you shoot off the meat of the stick, not the tip."

Debbie nodded again and skated in behind Amelia to wait her next turn.

"It must be cool to have your mom as the coach," Debbie said. "My mom can hardly skate." She glanced up at the stands where several parents, including Angie, sat beneath the heaters, talking and sipping their coffee.

Amelia shrugged. "It's all right. Sometimes it's a pain, though."

"But your mom is so awesome!"

Her teammate looked down. "Think about it, Deb," she said as they moved forward in the line. "Whatever she expects of the rest of you? She expects twice as much from me."

"Hey, you two, enough with the chatter. You can learn from your teammates' mistakes," Coach Mitch said, skating past.

"But I wish I could get some coaching at home. My dad coaches basketball," Debbie said, lowering her voice, "but he doesn't know much about hockey. And my mom, well, like I said, she doesn't even skate. And you should hear her if I forget to clean out my bag!" Debbie made her voice high and squeaky. "'I want that stuff put away as soon as you get home! And make sure you spray in there!' She is so boring."

"Amelia, you're up!" Coach Steph called. Amelia raised her eyebrows as if to say, "See what I mean?" before skating away.

At the end of practice Debbie collapsed on the bench in the dressing room. She closed her eyes and leaned back against the brick wall. Every single muscle in her body was tired. She longed for a hot bath and a really big plate of Angie's pancakes. A blast of air hit Debbie and she opened her eyes to see Coach Steph enter the dressing room. Deb sat up and slid over on the bench, making room in case Coach wanted to sit down.

Coach Steph remained standing. She looked at her clipboard, then at the girls spread around the room. "Just a few announcements."

Debbie slowly unlaced her skates, listening carefully. By the time the coach had finished speaking, Debbie was just shoving the last of her gear in her bag. Debbie scrambled to get up as Coach Steph clipped papers to her clipboard. They arrived at the door at the same time. Coach Steph pulled it open and motioned for Debbie to go through.

"Good practice today," she said. "Lots of hard work."

"Thanks. You make it easy to understand, you know, when you give suggestions and stuff," Deb said, hoping her words showed Coach Steph how much her encouragement meant.

"Well, thanks. I'm glad." Coach Steph smiled and started to move away.

"Have you been coaching a long time?" The coach turned back.

"About three years. I started coaching when Amelia wanted to play." She looked at Debbie, expectantly, but Debbie's mouth had gone dry. The dressing-room door opened and a wave of girls' voices washed over them.

"Do you like it?" Debbie blurted. "Coaching, I mean?"

"Yes, I do. Hockey is a great sport."

"Did you play as a kid?" Debbie asked, eyeing the approaching girls, praying they wouldn't stop to talk. They all waved and called goodbye and continued on their way. Debbie relaxed.

"I did. I started when I was about ten, I think," Coach Steph said. "I played with the boys for a long time because there weren't any girls' teams. You girls are lucky. Girls' hockey is so much more organized now — more teams, more leagues. Better coaches," she said with a grin.

Debbie's laugh was a little too loud, echoing off the stone walls. Clearing her throat, she said, "Maybe Amelia and I could practice together sometime. Maybe you can give us some extra pointers."

Coach Steph laughed and shook her head. Debbie's heart sank. "I'm always trying to give Amelia pointers, Deb. But she doesn't usually want my advice." She turned to Amelia, who had just joined them. "Do you, Pipsqueak?"

"It's just that you have so much of it, Mom," Amelia said. "And you give it so freely."

Debbie watched Amelia with her mother, and a knot of jealousy formed in her belly. Amelia didn't even appreciate what she had! If Debbie had a mother like Coach Steph, she wouldn't take her for granted.

Debbie wondered if Amelia was adopted. She didn't look anything like her mother. Steph was dark-haired with a dark complexion and dark blue eyes, while Amelia had fair hair, pale skin, and green eyes. In fact, Debbie realized, she herself, with her dark hair and dark eyes, looked more like Steph than Amelia did.

"Deb?" Angie's voice broke into her thoughts. "Ready to go?"

Debbie wasn't ready to go, and she hadn't finished talking with her coach. Why did people have to butt in where they weren't wanted? She glared at the side of Angie's head as her mom turned to speak to Coach Steph.

Then a thought occurred to her, and she turned to Amelia. "Wanna get together this week?" She spoke quickly before her chance was gone. Their mothers were already winding down their conversation.

"Sure. That'd be great, Deb. You want me just to walk home from school with you? Maybe Wednesday?" Amelia zipped up her coat and picked up the handle of her bag.

"Well …"

"Got everything, Deb?" her mom interrupted.

"Yes!" Deb snapped. She turned back to finish her conversation with Amelia, but she was already moving away.

"Bye, Deb, Angie," Coach Steph said with a little wave as she and Amelia headed for the doors.

Debbie followed them with her eyes until she could no longer see either of them.

41

Debbie heard the sound of a halting scale being played in her mom's studio when she came in the house Monday afternoon. She shushed Poker's enthusiastic barking and headed up to the kitchen, dropping her bag on the table and her shoes on the floor.

She poured herself a tall glass of grape juice and found a little cup of vanilla yogurt. She took both to the table and slid onto a chair, tucking her feet up under her. Poker sat beside her, watching hopefully as she lifted the spoon from the container to her mouth. Rifling around in her school bag, she found her hockey magazine and opened it. The pages and pages of player stats, team backgrounds, and play analysis fascinated Debbie. She could read them for hours.

She wondered if Coach Steph liked reading hockey magazines. Debbie bet she did. Coach Steph and Amelia probably sat looking through the stats together all the time. There was no way on earth her mother would sit and read this kind of thing with Debbie. Angie liked novels with bizarre covers and titles that made no sense. Greg read basketball magazines, but he was a high-school basketball coach, so he kind of had to.

Angie and Greg were so different! When Debbie stopped to think about it, she was actually surprised that her mom and dad were together at all. Greg was like Debbie — active, sporty. He liked to be doing things. And he didn't care if he messed up. Angie, on the other hand, was quiet and thoughtful, and did everything well. And if she couldn't do it almost perfectly, then she usually wouldn't try at all. Debbie wondered how they ever managed to get together in the first place.

The door to the studio opened and Debbie heard her mother saying goodbye to her student.

"Hi, there," Angie said, squeezing Debbie's shoulder as she passed. "How was your day? How did that math quiz go?"

"Okay. It was easier than I thought," Debbie said. She spooned the last of her yogurt into her mouth, then got up to rinse the container before dropping it in the recycling bin.

"Or maybe you were just well prepared for it," her mom suggested with a smile. "You worked hard, you knew the material."

Debbie returned the smile shyly. "Was that Marina playing the piano? She's sounding better. She must be practicing finally." Back in September, Debbie had escaped the house with Poker whenever little Marina came for her lesson.

"She is trying harder." Angie slid into a chair at the table and glanced at the open magazine. "This stuff really interests you, doesn't it? Greg enjoys reading this kind of magazine too. I'm more of a fiction person myself."

"Yeah, I'm going to take it for silent reading tomorrow," Debbie announced. "Mr. Joseph said I could read anything, even a magazine." She waited for her mom to object, but Angie just nodded.

"If you enjoy this sort of thing, then that's a good idea. It's better than sitting pretending to read for half an hour," she said. "Maybe we could check out the library and see if we can find any stories about hockey. You might enjoy those too."

"I guess. Maybe," Debbie said, a little surprised that her mother wasn't lecturing her on what she should be reading.

"Listen, Deb, there's something I wanted to discuss with you," Angie said. She rifled through a stack of papers and pulled out a pale green pamphlet. "I've been trying to think of things you and I could do together. Something we'd both enjoy. Knowing how active you like to be, I wondered if you might be interested in trying a yoga class."

"Yoga?" Debbie had a sudden mental picture of being bent into some impossible position, and she smirked.

"Yes, yoga. It's very good exercise and extremely helpful for developing flexibility and strength. You'd probably find it very beneficial for hockey." Angie held out the pamphlet.

"I'm not sure about yoga, Mom," Debbie said, taking the paper. The cover showed a woman sitting cross-legged on a mat, her eyes closed, her hands resting on her knees, fingers pointing skyward. "Isn't it all about breathing and meditation and chanting?"

"Some forms of yoga concentrate on those things," Angie said with a smile. "This isn't that kind of yoga, though. This class I'm looking at for us is more about strength and learning the poses properly. It's not easy, but I think you'd enjoy the challenge."

"I'm not sure."

"I'd like to give it a try. We can go to one class for free to see what we think, and then decide whether we want to sign up."

Debbie met her mom's eyes and sighed. "I'll try one class."

"That's all I'm asking. Now, my next student will be here any second. Will you start cutting up the vegetables for a stir-fry? And cook some rice? I've already started marinating the chicken." Angie got up from the table and put the pamphlet by the phone. "Thank you, Deb," she said.

As soon as her mother had closed the door of her studio, Debbie went to the phone.

"Amelia? It's Deb Lowell," she said when her teammate answered.

"Hi, Deb. What's up?"

"Well, I'm really sorry, but you can't come over Wednesday after school." Debbie's heart pounded and she gripped the phone tighter so it wouldn't slip from her fingers.

"Why? What happened?"

"My mom has students and she doesn't like me having people over when she's teaching. I forgot to tell you before."

"Oh," Amelia said. "I was really looking forward to coming."

"I know! It sucks. But I don't know what we can do …" Come on, Amelia, she silently pushed.

"Well, what if you came here instead?"

Debbie let out her breath in relief. "Really? Would that be okay with your mom?"

"Hold on a second and I'll go ask."

Debbie grinned to herself and gave Poker an extra-enthusiastic ear rubbing to celebrate when Amelia came back to say it was all set.

5 Game Plan

"Do you know where this address is?" Debbie held up the slip of paper with Amelia's address written on it. Her dad took it, squinting at the tiny writing.

"Who wrote this?" he asked, reaching for his glasses. "Tinkerbell?"

"You're just getting old." Debbie took another bite of her sandwich, wiping jelly from her lips with the back of her hand.

"Not exactly. Go use MapQuest," her dad suggested, taking his glasses off again. "Who lives there?"

"A girl on my team, Amelia Larsen."

"I didn't know you two were friends. She's the coach's daughter, isn't she?"

"So? Can't I be friends with the coach's daughter?"

Greg raised his eyebrows. "Whoa, there," he said, holding up his hands to fend off Debbie's attack. "I was just asking."

Red-faced, Debbie muttered an apology. She finished

her sandwich and stood up. "We're going to hang together," she explained as she headed for the stairs. She was careful to keep her tone neutral. "And maybe practice a bit."

"Don't forget to put those dishes in the dishwasher," he said. Debbie rolled her eyes as she turned back and cleaned up her dishes before going upstairs to the computer.

★ ★ ★

Debbie dropped her bike and stick on the driveway and went up the cracked walk to the front door. A hockey net, several battered sticks, and a puck lay scattered across the front lawn. A grin spread across Debbie's face. She must have the right house.

Coach Steph answered her knock.

"Deb! Hi," she said, standing back to let Debbie step in. "Come on in. Amelia's in the kitchen."

Debbie added her shoes to the pile in the hallway and followed her coach up a few stairs and into the kitchen. The counters were strewn with dirty measuring cups and spoons, spilled batter, and opened containers. Amelia was sitting at the counter amid the mess, eating. The scent of apple filled the room and Debbie's stomach rumbled.

"Hey, Deb," Amelia said, around a mouthful of apple spice muffin.

Coach Steph moved around the island to where a rack of muffins sat cooling. "Would you like a muffin, Deb?"

"Sure, thanks." Debbie climbed up on the tall chair beside Amelia. She thought of the kitchen at home, where things were washed and put away almost before they were used. Debbie imagined her mom's reaction to Coach Steph's kitchen and a giggle escaped her.

"What's so funny?" Amelia asked.

Debbie clamped her lips together and swallowed hard. "I was just thinking of a really dumb joke I heard at school today," she blurted.

Amelia looked at her expectantly. Darn it, Debbie thought, scrambling to think of a joke. "Why was six afraid of seven?" she said.

"I don't know."

"Because seven 'ate' nine."

Amelia groaned and her mom laughed. "That was bad, Deb," Coach Steph said, shaking her head.

"I'll say," agreed Amelia. "You better stick to hockey."

Debbie grinned and popped the last of her muffin in her mouth. Amelia slid off her chair, brushing crumbs to the floor. "Wanna go to my room?" she suggested.

"Where should I put my plate?"

Amelia waved her off. "Just leave it."

As they left the kitchen, Amelia turned to Debbie. "So what's up with you and Paige?" she asked.

Debbie's heart did a funny leap in her chest. "Nothing, why?"

Amelia shrugged. "I don't know, you just usually

hang out with Paige after school."

"Is there something wrong with making new friends?" Debbie demanded.

"No, of course not," Amelia sputtered. "I was just curious."

They went up a curved staircase, swerving around piles of books and papers, and along a hallway. "That's my brother Aaron's bedroom," Amelia explained as they went. "He's nine and a pain. Be very thankful you don't have any brothers, Deb. And that's my parents' bedroom. When we were having this house built, my mom insisted on having a soaker tub put in their bathroom. It's amazing. I use it after practice and games. And that room is one of the guest rooms — we have two. Not that we have tons of company or anything."

Debbie's thoughts turned back to Paige. Paige was a talker too, Debbie acknowledged. But at least she said something interesting once in a while.

"My dad's office is downstairs, but Mom has a small one up here. She works as a consultant for professional teams, helping players play better or get over injuries and that kind of thing. And this," she said with a small dramatic flourish, "is my room."

Debbie stepped inside, set her pack down on the thick tan carpet with a muffled thud, and walked across to the window. The room was bigger than Debbie's and, she quickly noticed, much tidier than the rest of the house. Amelia had a double bed, a dresser and bedside table, a large desk with her own computer, and a picture window that looked over the backyard. High up on one wall was a shelf lined with dolls dressed in fancy clothes, their porcelain faces staring out blankly.

"It's real nice, Amelia. You sure have a lot of dolls."

Amelia climbed up on her desk chair and reached for one of the dolls. "My Granny brought me this back from England. Isn't she gorgeous? She's my favourite. It's my collection."

Debbie perched on the edge of the bed.

"Do you collect anything, Deb?" Amelia replaced the English doll carefully. She straightened the skirt of another doll, then climbed down from her chair.

"Naw."

"I love collecting. You should think of something to collect," Amelia suggested, sitting beside Debbie. "What about stickers? Or — oh, I know! My friend Janelle collects butterflies. She's got butterfly jewellery, figurines, even a butterfly mirror!"

"I don't think I'm a collecting person."

"Oh, well, sure."

Silence filled the room. Debbie stared out the window, wondering where Coach Steph had gone. It was a big house. With the bedroom door closed, all sound from outside the room disappeared.

"What do you want to do?" Amelia asked finally. "We've got some cool video games or we could …"

"Well, I brought my stick," Debbie interrupted,

standing. "I thought we could practice."

A crease appeared between Amelia's blond eyebrows. "Practice hockey? Outside? Like, in the driveway?"

"Well, yeah." Debbie moved toward the door. "What's the big deal?"

"Umm, I'm not sure."

"Don't you want to play better? Score some more goals? Come on, I have to go home at five," Debbie said, pulling at Amelia's shirt.

Downstairs Debbie found Coach Steph in the kitchen, chopping vegetables. "What's up?" she asked, looking up as the girls came through.

"We're going to practice outside for a bit," Debbie explained. "Work on our shots."

"Good idea. Remember to follow through with your stick."

"Yeah, yeah," Amelia said, grabbing Debbie's elbow.

Debbie pulled away. "Amelia, I want to hear what your mom has to say."

"Tell you what," Coach Steph said, sliding carrots into a bowl, "just let me finish getting these vegetables ready, and I'll come out with you."

Amelia groaned. "Now see what you've done?" she muttered as the girls went to put on their shoes. But Debbie couldn't help grinning. Sometimes things just had a way of working out.

6 Flexibility

The yoga class was in the basement studio of the instructor's home. Judging from the size of the house, teaching yoga paid well, Debbie decided. On the Saturday morning, theirs was the only car in front of the house, though, so maybe they were the only students. *Wouldn't that be perfect*, Debbie thought. No one to hide behind. Rule number one, always sit at least two rows back so you are out of the teacher's line of sight.

"Is she a Yogi?" Debbie asked as she and Angie got out of the car.

Angie laughed but shook her head. "I don't think so. But her name is Rielle."

Rielle? What kind of name was that?

They went up the driveway, then followed a series of signs pointing around to the left of the garage. At the back of the house was a door with a sign on it: Inner Harmony Yoga Studio — Welcome. Angie looked at Debbie and they both shrugged as Angie turned the doorknob.

"Here goes," Angie muttered.

Debbie's stomach started twisting and jumping, and she swallowed hard as she and her mom headed inside.

"Come in, come in. I'm Rielle," a small woman said, meeting them at the door. She wore black tights and a purple T-shirt, and the dark hair tied back in a ponytail was streaked with gray. "You must be Angie and Debbie. Welcome to Inner Harmony."

She stepped forward and shook Angie's hand, then reached for Debbie's. Her grasp was firm and dry, confident. "You can leave your things in the baskets. Once class starts, I lock this outside door, so feel free to put your purses in the baskets too. Did you bring your own mats and belts? No? That's fine — everything you need is in the studio. Slip off your socks and come on through."

The studio itself wasn't all that large. Another woman and a young girl were already there, sitting cross-legged on mats on the floor.

"Angie, Deb," Rielle said, following them in, "this is Cass," pointing to the girl, "and her mother Janine."

At least I'm not the only kid in the class, Debbie thought thankfully, offering up a small wave.

Rielle pointed to some shelves by the door where piles of blankets, stacks of blocks, and some rolled mats were kept. "Help yourself to a mat," she said. "I'd also suggest taking a couple of blocks, maybe two blankets, and a belt as well."

Debbie stuck close to her mother as they gathered their things and found spots on the floor. She unrolled her mat directly behind Angie's, then sat down and picked at her big toe as she looked around the room. The walls were painted in pale colours and the floor was wood. It was a peaceful room, which Debbie guessed was the intention. There were no pictures on the walls and it was very quiet. Too quiet, Debbie thought, squirming. Couldn't they do yoga to music?

Rielle shut the door. She crossed the floor to her own mat at the front of the room, sat down on the little lift of blankets, and crossed her legs. "It looks as though we're just five today. So let's get started," she said in her soft voice. "Let's start by centring ourselves. Sit in *Sukhasana* — easy crossed legs. Make sure your weight is evenly spread between the two sit bones."

Laughter bubbled up inside her and Debbie struggled to keep a straight face as she followed Rielle's instructions — or rather, as she tried to follow Rielle's instructions. Sit bones? Sacrum? Perineum? What were those things? Where were those things?

"Let's take *Balasana* — child's pose," Rielle told them, kneeling. She explained what she was doing as she bent in half, arms along her legs, forehead resting on the mat.

Debbie folded herself into child's pose and stared at the dark mat beneath her head, wondering what exactly she was doing there. She could have been hanging with Paige or practicing her slapshots in the driveway. But, no, she was about to lift her hips to the ceiling while she pushed her shoulders away from her ears and let her head hang loose between her arms.

"*Dandasana* or downward dog is a great warm-up pose," Rielle said. Debbie stifled another giggle. At least the name fit the pose — Poker did exactly what Rielle was doing when he stretched, except he usually yawned and often farted at the same time.

"Yoga is all about being symmetrical." Rielle stood up and moved around the room as she spoke. "We're trying to achieve balance, symmetry. Try to free your mind of outside distractions and concentrate only on your body. The more you practice yoga, the more your body remembers the poses, remembers how the poses feel."

The voice stopped moving and all of a sudden Debbie felt a light, feathery touch on her hip. She stiffened. "Relax," the instructor said. "Don't worry about your heels touching the mat, Deb. Concentrate instead on reaching with your hips to the ceiling. No, don't hunch up your shoulders." The feather touched the tops of Debbie's shoulders until she eased them back. "Let your head hang, nice and relaxed. That's it! Good, good. Can you feel the difference?"

Debbie couldn't feel anything except that her body didn't want to move in about six different directions all at the same time, but she nodded anyway. She sneaked a peek at her mom. Angie seemed to be having no trouble with this push-pull-reach-stretch-relax-don't-think stuff. It figured.

They came out of downward dog and stood in mountain pose for a few minutes, stretching their shoulders. Then, all of a sudden, they were trees — one leg up, foot pressing against inner thigh of other leg, hands high in the air. Debbie tried focusing on a spot on the wall in front of her to balance, but as soon as she lifted her leg she toppled over like a child's block tower. It didn't help that her mom seemed to have perfect balance and stood looking like a tree, arms stretched high over her head.

"Try using the wall, Deb," Rielle suggested. "Or don't bring your foot up as high. Rest it on your calf instead. *Vrikshasana* is a wonderful pose requiring lots of concentration. It's not about mastering the pose as much as your *intention* of mastering the pose."

Except no one else had to use the wall or put her foot on her calf instead of her thigh. Debbie shook her head and tried again, only to fall to the mat. Hot, frustrated anger bubbled inside her.

"Let's try the other side," Rielle directed. Debbie watched as her mother, with apparent lack of effort, raised her left foot, placed it against her right thigh, lifted her arms to the heavens, and stood — like a tree or whatever — barely moving.

Debbie glared at her spot on the wall, leaned to the right, and lifted her left leg, bending her knee. She got her foot against her thigh, tipping and swaying like a baby trying to walk. She stayed upright, though, and slowly raised her arms. Then she tipped over.

In the car on the way home, Debbie stared out the window. After they had driven a couple of blocks, her mom reached over and squeezed Debbie's leg.

"I'm sorry that first time was a bit challenging for you. Rielle had assured me this session was geared for beginners."

"You didn't have any trouble with any of it," Debbie blurted, yanking her leg away from her mother's hand.

"I have done yoga a bit in the past, Deb. But I'm no expert. Some of those poses challenged me too."

Debbie snorted. "Not from where I stood."

"Exactly what are you angry about, Deb?" Angie asked. "Are you angry because I didn't struggle, or are you angry because you did? It was your first time. You didn't expect to be perfect at it, did you?"

Debbie opened her mouth to say no, then closed it again. She had expected it to be easy. A beginner's yoga class — how hard could that be? But it had been hard. Her muscles weren't used to the poses. She wasn't very flexible. Her balance was lousy.

"Listen, sweetie," her mom began, "don't be so hard on yourself. The more you practice yoga, the easier it will become. You'll get more flexible, and the poses will come more easily for you."

Debbie didn't answer.

"You just have to give it a chance."

Angie pulled into the Lowell's driveway. The garage door was open. Inside, Greg had the hood of his car up. He straightened up and waved as they drove up.

"You said we'd try it once and see what we thought," Debbie reminded her mother. "I've tried it once and I didn't like it. I don't want to go again." She looked at Angie, daring her mother to challenge her.

Instead Angie seemed to collapse in on herself. She reached up and wiped at her eyes.

"Did you get something in your eye?" Debbie asked.

"No," Angie said, fingering her car keys. "I'm fine."

7 Breakaway

Debbie came downstairs Sunday morning to find her dad already at the table, sipping his coffee. She grabbed a cereal bar and a juice box, and leaned against the counter to eat her pre-practice breakfast.

"You taking me to practice this morning?" she asked.

"Yup. Lucky you," Greg said, setting his empty mug in the sink. "Ready?"

"I guess. Mom finally sick of spending an hour in the cold?" Debbie asked as they headed to the garage. Her dad slipped into his boots and jacket without answering.

Once they were in the van, heaters blowing warm air at them, Debbie leaned back and closed her eyes. "I never did understand why Mom insisted on taking me to practice every week. I mean, she doesn't even like hockey." Debbie snorted. "Guess she finally wised up."

"You know, Deb," her dad said quietly, "you might

cut your mother a little slack."

Debbie opened her eyes and turned to look at him. "What's that supposed to mean?" she demanded.

"You maybe don't realize," he said slowly, as though considering his words carefully, "how often you put her down."

"I don't put Mom down! I just tease her. Like you tease me. I thought that's what families did."

"Hold on, back up," Greg said. He stopped at an intersection and turned to face Debbie. His usually easy-going manner was serious. "There's a difference between teasing someone and insulting them. I hear you, Deb. You're very negative when you speak to Mom."

Debbie tried to interrupt, to defend herself, but her dad put up a hand to stop her. "Like just now. When you discovered I was taking you to practice, you immediately assumed she was sick of sitting in the cold. You didn't even show concern."

Debbie squirmed in her seat, anxious to be at the rink. She looked out the windshield and saw yet another red glowing light ahead of them. She blew out a hard breath. "Okay. Why isn't Mom taking me to practice?"

The light changed and Greg pulled forward. The darkened streets were almost deserted as they drove. The only sound was the faint swish of tires on damp pavement.

"Your mom needed a break."

"See, I was right …"

"Not from hockey practice, Deb. From you."

"Me? What have I done?" Debbie's voice was loud in the quiet car.

Greg turned into the parking lot of the ice complex and found a parking spot. He turned off the ignition. "She's trying really hard to be a good mom to you, Deb. But you don't make it easy sometimes. I think this morning she just felt like she needed some time to herself."

Feelings tore through Debbie, none of which she understood. She climbed out of the van and met Greg at the back. He'd already hauled her bag out and set it down on the ground. Their hands met as Debbie reached to grab the handle. He squeezed Debbie's fingers.

"Being a mom is hard work, and Angie is still pretty new to it. You might want to take it easy on her once in a while."

Debbie blinked twice, then headed for the doors. The rest of her teammates were already in the dressing room when she came in.

"Morning, Deb," Meghan called. "You look like you aren't awake yet. Big night?"

A sprinkle of laughter filled the room. Debbie forced a grin as she sat down. "Something like that."

"Did you hear about that party at Carsen Miller's

place last night?" someone asked. "The cops were called in and everything."

"Carsen Miller is so hot," Vanessa said with a deep sigh.

"Knows it too," Meghan muttered. "He's gone out with most of the grade eight girls at our school. And broken up with most of them too."

"Well, he's still hot," Vanessa insisted, standing.

Debbie finished suiting up. She leaned back against the wall, thinking about what her dad had said in the car. Was she really negative with her mom? How did you know when it wasn't teasing anymore? Little prickles of guilt poked at her insides. She didn't mean to hurt her mom's feelings. Maybe Angie was being oversensitive.

She grabbed her stick from the row by the door and headed out to the ice. Once the team had warmed up, Coach Steph whistled them in.

"Take a knee!" she said, and everyone dropped to one knee on the ice.

"I'd rather take a nap," Vanessa whispered to Debbie.

"I hear you," Debbie replied, nodding.

"Girls! Attention here, please!" Coach Steph shot a warning glance at Debbie and Vanessa. "Our game against Chilliwack this week is going to be a tough one. We need to spend this practice tightening up some areas where we have been outworked and out-thought." She checked her notes and then looked up, eyeing each player thoughtfully.

"Mitch, I want you to take Amelia, Deb, Meghan, Charlie, Kira, and Hannah," she began. Quickly the rest of the players were divided up.

Debbie stood up at the sound of her name. When their group was assembled, they skated after Coach Mitch to the far end of the rink.

"A little three-on-three this morning, ladies," he told them. "Meghan, you take centre. Deb, right wing. Amelia, left. Hannah, Charlie, I want some good defence in front of Kira in goal. Hannah, you cover Deb. Charlie, you cover Amelia."

Kira skated for the net. Charlie and Hannah skated backward in front of their goalie. Debbie, Amelia, and Meghan took up their positions. Meghan dropped the puck in front of her stick. Debbie skated toward the boards. She kept one eye on Hannah, the other on the puck, waiting for Meghan's pass. Debbie caught it mid-stride, right on the tape. Hannah was right there, crowding in, doing everything but physically touching Debbie.

Coach Mitch blew his whistle and they all went back to their positions to do it again. "Deb, let's get a bit more speed going," he suggested. "It's easier to out-maneuver a defender if you've got your legs going. The Chilliwack players are quick, so you're going to have to skate hard Tuesday night. Good job, Hannah. Okay, let's do it again!"

Coach Mitch hadn't been exaggerating when he'd said the Chilliwack Chargers were quick. They never seemed to run out of gas! Debbie let out an exhausted breath as the linesman called offside. Slowly she skated into position for the face-off. Barely ten minutes into the first period and the Lightning were already struggling. The Chargers had ten shots on goal. "It's a good thing our goalie is doing her job tonight," Debbie muttered as the puck dropped.

Amelia won the draw and dished the puck to Debbie. She circled the Lightning net and headed up-ice along the boards. A Chargers defender stick-checked her before she got out of the zone, and the puck got trapped between their skates. Debbie tried to jam it free, but a Chargers forward scooped in and stole it. Charlie skated in hard and angled the forward into the boards, digging for the puck.

"Deb!" she hollered, finally skating free.

Debbie moved to centre ice. She caught Charlie's pass on the fly and skated hard. Amelia and Vanessa raced up-ice. Debbie felt the breath of the Chargers defender hot on her neck. Seeing a chance for a breakaway, Debbie passed off the puck to Vanessa. Vanessa caught it and went for the slapshot.

The puck flew through the five-hole between the goalie's legs and came to rest in the back of the net. Cheers erupted from the Lightning bench and from the few parents gathered to watch.

Debbie and her line headed to the bench for a fly-by, their grins almost splitting their faces.

"That was really well-played, girls," Coach Steph told them, beaming. "Deb — that was an awesome move. Your head was up, so you saw the chance. That's smart hockey. Excellent job, girls."

Coach Steph's final words were meant for the whole line, but as she spoke, she was looking at Debbie.

8 Camping Out

"Deb, if you aren't out of bed yet, time to get up and have a shower," Angie called from the kitchen early Friday morning.

"I'm up!"

Debbie looked around at the mess of clothes and belongings scattered all over the floor and frowned. Where had she put her new camp uniform? She pawed through the things spilling out of the backpack and lifted her new sleeping bag. Finally she found what she was looking for on her desk chair.

"Deb?" Angie appeared at the bedroom doorway. "Paige is on the phone."

"Oh, thanks," Debbie said. "Can I take it up here?"

"Keep it short — you haven't eaten breakfast and you need to get in the shower." Her mother headed back downstairs.

"Yeah, yeah …" Debbie headed for her parents' bedroom. "Hey, Paige," she said into the phone, flopping down on her parents' neatly made bed.

"Did you remember to get the comics? And a deck of cards?"

"Yeah. Did you remember —"

"Yeah, I remembered!"

"You don't even know what I was going to ask," Debbie objected.

"Of course I know what you were going to ask. You've only asked me three times!"

"It hasn't been three times," Debbie argued as Poker bounded into the bedroom. He spotted Debbie and trotted toward her, sitting at her feet expectantly. "But did you —"

"YES! I got the marshmallows, graham crackers, and chocolate!"

"Okay, okay. I'll see you in a while. I've got to have a — Oh, Pokes! No!" she cried as Poker jumped on the bed beside her, nuzzling his nose under her arm.

"What happened?" Paige asked, alarmed.

"Poker just jumped up on the bed. My mom will kill him!" Debbie pushed at the excited dog. "Get off, silly! I've got to go, Paige. I'll see you in a while."

Debbie dove at Poker, but he jumped out of the way. He lowered his head and chest, tail high in the air, and barked at her.

"No, I'm not playing with you!" Debbie lunged for him again. Poker jumped down and scurried out of the room. Debbie crawled off the messed-up bed, her shoulders slumped. Her mother's bed was in shambles. She pulled at the duvet, smoothing the wrinkles and straightening the pillows. Then she grabbed her clothes and headed into her parents' bathroom.

Twenty minutes later, dressed, hair dried and tied back into a ponytail, Debbie made her way into the kitchen. Greg was still at the table, finishing his coffee. He looked up as she came in and smiled.

"That uniform looks good," he told her.

"Thanks. Sure glad the weather is good. I wasn't looking forward to camping in the rain." Debbie slid into her chair. She reached for the milk and poured some into her bowl of cereal.

"It is still cold, though, Deb," her mom reminded her. "Be sure to pack some extra socks and —"

"Yeah, yeah," Debbie interrupted, her mouth full of cereal. "I've got extra everything."

"I'm just going to finish getting dressed," her mom said. "When you've finished eating, please straighten your room and get your things downstairs so we can load the van. Paige will be here in twenty minutes."

Debbie lifted the bowl and drained the last of the milk and cereal into her mouth. She set the bowl down and wiped the drips from her chin. Then she caught her dad's raised eyebrows.

"Good thing your mom didn't see that, Deb," he said. He took his own dishes to the counter and loaded them into the dishwasher.

"Deb?" Angie called from upstairs. "Can you come up here, please? Now."

Debbie exchanged glances with Greg and headed upstairs. Her mom was standing just inside the master bedroom, her hands on her hips. Debbie approached warily.

"What happened in here?" Angie waved at the dishevelled bed.

"What? I straightened the covers." It looked fine to Debbie.

"I've asked you not to use the phone in here, Deb. There's one in the office you can use."

"Sorry," Debbie muttered and pulled at the edge of the duvet.

"And one other thing," Angie continued, her voice stopping Debbie as she moved toward the door. "If you are going to use our bathroom to shower, could you please pick up after yourself?"

Debbie looked around the bathroom, a small frown on her face. So she had forgotten to hang up her towel. And so what if the shampoo container lay leaking on the floor of the shower stall. So strands of dark hair littered the counter, and the cap hadn't been replaced on the toothpaste tube. What was the big deal? She stepped in the room and quickly tidied her things.

"There," she said when she'd finished. "Satisfied?"

Her mother's eyes narrowed and her lips pursed.

"There is no need to be rude. You used my space and left it a mess. It's bad enough your own room is a constant disaster. I will not have you treating my spaces in the same disrespectful manner."

"I'm sorry! If you'd wanted a perfect daughter, you should have picked some other kid!" Debbie glowered at her mother.

"I don't want a perfect daughter and I don't want 'some other kid'," Angie said. She tucked a strand of hair behind her ear and sighed. "I want the daughter I have, a daughter I love, to be respectful. And a bit tidier. Will you try, please?"

Debbie muttered, "Yes."

"Fine. Thank you. Go and finish getting ready. I'll meet you downstairs in a few minutes."

Back in her own room, Debbie stuffed the last of her things in her backpack, jammed her pillow on top, and somehow managed to get it closed. She put the pack and her sleeping bag out in the hall, and turned back to the disaster of her room. She would never, ever be as tidy as Angie. There were way more important things to think about than how straight the covers were on the bed.

Wouldn't Mom love having Amelia for a daughter, Debbie thought as she picked up the clothes from the floor and threw them in the laundry basket in the closet. Then she grabbed her camping things and dragged them downstairs.

★ ★ ★

"We should be coming up to it," Angie said, peering through the windshield. "Diana said the sign is hard to see."

Towering Douglas firs rose on either side of the narrow road. Amelia, Paige, and Debbie all watched carefully out their windows for the sign announcing the camp.

"Oh, there it is!" Paige called out.

Angie signalled and turned down a gravel driveway, coming out of the trees into a small parking lot. In front of them, a long, single-storey lodge was nestled into the trees. Several other vans were already there, and girls milled about, sleeping bags and backpacks lying in abandoned piles everywhere.

The Lowells' van had barely come to a stop when the doors slid open and the girls spilled out, their excited voices adding to the noise.

"Don't disappear without your gear!" Angie called after them as she headed around to the back of the van.

Diana and Mizuki stood amongst the chaos with their clipboards, talking to parents. Diana's camp hat was so filled with badges, pins, and shrink art that Debbie couldn't even see a hint of the original blue. She touched a hand to her own bare hat. Well, almost bare, she reminded herself, fingering the one badge — a gift from her mom — pinned there.

"I thought you might like to have something on your hat," Angie had said the night before while she and Debbie packed. "This was one of my first camp badges." The circular crest depicted tiny brown huts nestled among a deep green forest. Along the bottom were the words *Camp Olave 1976*.

"Okay, ladies, listen up!" Diana called out. "Grab your gear, find your groups, and go claim a tent. You've got fifteen minutes to get your tents set up, and then I want everyone in the mess hall."

Angie helped Debbie load her heavy backpack onto her back, adjusting the wide shoulder straps until they sat comfortably. Then she gave Debbie her sleeping bag. "I'm going to leave now," she said. "Have fun."

"Yeah, okay, bye."

Angie hugged her and kissed her forehead. "See you Sunday," she said as she climbed into the van.

Debbie, Amelia, and Paige followed the others down a small hill and through the trees out to a large clearing. In front of them were seven square ridgepole tents, their weathered grey canvas roofs covered with blue tarps.

"That's where we're sleeping?" Debbie muttered, glancing back longingly at the snug lodge.

Other groups had already claimed four of the tents, so Paige led them to the last one in the semicircle. "It's closest to the mess hall!" she declared.

"I think I'd rather be closer to the bathrooms,"

Amelia said.

Paige dropped to her knees and shoved her things to the back of the tent. Amelia climbed in next and claimed the middle, so Debbie dropped her stuff just inside the flap that served as a door. The worn wooden planks that made up the floor were hard under her knees. She was glad Angie had bought her a thick foam mattress to put under her sleeping bag. She pulled that out first and unrolled it, then unrolled her sleeping bag and laid it on top.

"You don't roll in your sleep, do you, Deb?" Paige asked. "You'll roll right out the door if you do."

"It is small. Can you imagine if there were four of us?"

"Do either of you snore?" Amelia asked.

"I was worried you guys might snore," Debbie confessed with a grin, ducking the rolled-up socks Paige aimed at her head. She grabbed them and tossed them back, beaning Paige squarely in the back of the head.

"Hey!" Paige cried, lobbing another one, which hit Amelia on the nose.

"Don't turn your back during a sock fight!" Debbie yelled.

"No fair, I can't find my socks!"

"Not our problem, Amelia. Ouch! Oh you're going to pay for that one, Deb!" Paige crawled across the mess of sleeping bags, carrying a handful of socks.

She bombarded Debbie with them — striped ones, woollen ones, even a pair of socks with toes.

Debbie was laughing so hard she was afraid she'd wet her pants. Out of socks, she put her hands over her face and tried to ward off the attack from Paige and Amelia. None of the girls heard the knock on the tent frame.

"What on earth?"

"Oh, hi, Diana," Paige said, spitting her red curls out of her mouth. She cleared her throat and sat up.

Debbie struggled to sit up as well. Half of her sleeping bag had fallen out of the tent. With a guilty glance at Diana, she pulled it inside and brushed it off.

"We were just, you know, unpacking," Amelia explained, holding up a pair of socks.

"So I see. Well," Diana said, "when you're done 'unpacking,' everyone is signing up for jobs in the dining hall."

Diana let the tent flap fall back in place. The three girls listened as her footsteps faded away, and then their stifled giggles exploded.

★ ★ ★

"I really, really appreciate my dishwasher at home," Amelia griped as she took another pot from Debbie to dry. "REALLY appreciate it."

The small kitchen was littered with the dinner dishes. Through the pass-through, Debbie could see Paige sweeping the wood floor, the chairs already neatly stacked on the tables.

"Well, we're the dishwashers here. If you hadn't started a sock fight, we wouldn't have been left with the lousy jobs," Debbie reminded her.

"I didn't start the sock fight!" Amelia cried. "Paige did." She set a dry pot on its shelf and picked up another one.

"Whatever. Here — dry this one too."

"Wash it first," Amelia told her, handing it back.

"It's clean!"

"No, it's not. Look, right there," Amelia said, pointing at a piece of noodle stuck to the side of the pot. "If you're going to do the job, do it right."

"Whatever!" Debbie said, flicking water at Amelia's face.

"Hey!" Amelia dipped her hand in the soapy dishwater and flicked it at Debbie. Debbie ducked, grabbing at Amelia's hands as soapsuds and water flew around the kitchen, soaking the floor as well as the dishwashers.

They were giggling so hard, neither girl heard Paige come up behind them. "What's going on?" she asked. "I said, what's going on?!"

Debbie and Amelia stopped wrestling and stared at Paige. They looked at each other and started giggling again. "Nothing, really. Right, Amelia?" Debbie said, letting go of Amelia's wet T-shirt.

"No, we're good," Amelia added, clearing her

throat. She grabbed a dry dishtowel from the drawer and went back to the dishes, but giggles kept escaping her. She elbowed Debbie who elbowed her back.

"And you're not going to let me in on the joke?" Paige huffed.

"There's nothing to let you in on," Debbie told her without turning around.

"That's the last pot," Debbie said, handing it to Amelia. She let the water out of the sink and dried her hands. "Is it campfire time?" she asked as the three girls left the kitchen. "'Cause I want some s'mores!"

"You aren't hungry again, are you?" Amelia held her stomach. "How can you be hungry after all the spaghetti you ate at dinner?"

"It was really good spaghetti! And, besides, you have been going on about these stupid s'mores for so long, I'm just about going crazy waiting to try them. You coming, Paige?" she called over her shoulder.

Outside, the dark had settled over the campsite like a blanket, the only electric light coming from the mess hall. From inside the tents, the eerie yellow glow of flashlights bounced and rolled across the canvas roofs.

Paige and Amelia disappeared inside the tent, but Debbie stayed outside. The trees were dark looming shadows, closing in on all sides, leaving only a small circle of sky exposed. But when she looked up into that circle, it seemed as though every star in the sky twinkled back at her. It was so beautiful and peaceful it made Debbie's throat ache.

In the middle of a circle of wooden benches, the campfire crackled and hissed, its brilliant ruby flames dancing. Slowly the girls came from their tents, drawn by the heat and light of the fire. Debbie found a spot on one of the benches and saved a seat on either side of her for Amelia and Paige. She tucked her hands in her pockets and thought briefly about going back to the tent to get her gloves, but the fire held her mesmerized.

When everyone had found a spot to sit, Diana began to sing, her voice steady and strong. "Fire's burning, fire's burning./ Draw nearer, draw nearer,/ in the gloaming, in the gloaming,/ come sing and be merry," she sang. When she came to the end she began again, and then Mizuki joined her, their voices floating together.

Diana showed them all how to sing the round and got them started. One by one, the small groups began until all their voices were singing the simple words of welcome. Around and around they went, the night air carrying their voices away. Paige linked her arm through Debbie's, Debbie linked hers with Amelia's, and all three swayed as they sang.

At the end of the round the girls cheered and clapped. "We should go on tour!" someone called out and everyone laughed.

"What's a 'gloaming' anyway, Diana?" someone else asked.

"Gloaming is twilight or dusk," Diana explained. "We're a bit past that now, but you get the idea."

"Can we sing something else?" Debbie asked.

"Absolutely. How about something a bit more fun. Any suggestions?"

"Oh, oh! 'Down by the Bay'!" Kelsie cried out.

Debbie listened carefully as the other Pathfinders began.

"Down by the bay,/ where the watermelons grow,/ back to my home/ I dare not go!/ For if I do,/ my mother will say ..." the girls sang.

"Did you ever see llamas wearing striped pajamas?" Diana called out.

Amid the raucous laughter, they began again. As they sang, each girl took a turn throwing out some ridiculous suggestion. "You're next, Deb," Mizuki called out.

Frantically Debbie scrambled to come up with something, but by that time all the easy animals had been done. Then it hit her.

"Did you ever see an anaconda driving in a Honda?" she asked.

"Good one!" Diana said as the others laughed.

When they'd exhausted "Down by the Bay" there was a sudden lull.

"When do we eat?" someone called.

Diana pulled a bag of marshmallows out from behind her and waved them above her head to a chorus of cheers. "Find a stick then come see me," she instructed, ripping open the bag.

Paige had coached Debbie and Amelia on the best way to roast marshmallows. Debbie crouched next to the fire and set her stick in the glowing embers. Slowly she turned the stick until every inch of her marshmallow was a golden brown. She blew on it gently as she grabbed two graham crackers and a square of chocolate. Carefully she slid the marshmallow off the stick between the crackers and squeezed everything together.

"Okay," she announced, "here goes!"

"Wait for a second!" Paige told her. "Let the chocolate melt a bit — it's even better then."

Debbie took a big bite and a smile spread across her lips as the flavours exploded in her mouth. "Thish ish weally goo …" she said and shoved the rest in her mouth before reaching for another marshmallow.

9 Change of Plans

It was Sunday afternoon. The girls had pretty much finished cleaning up by the time the first of the parents arrived. Debbie swept the last bits of dirt and fir needles out of the tent, and then leaned on the broom as she looked out the opening at the campground before her.

She wished they were staying longer. Despite the cold weather, it had been a great weekend. On Saturday they'd gone on a long hike, made some cool twig picture frames, created some of their own shrink art for their camp hats, and made banana boats by the campfire. There was even talk of coming back in August and doing some canoeing on Whonnock Lake.

Debbie grabbed her pack and sleeping bag, and headed for the row of cars already collected in the parking lot. They'd have a blast on the way home, and maybe, if she were crafty enough, she'd get the front seat next to Coach Steph.

She was headed for Coach Steph's van when she

heard her name being called. Turning, she saw her mom.

"Hi, sweetie!"

"I thought I was going home with Coach Steph," Deb said, glancing back at her friends.

"You were supposed to. But there was a slight change of plans, so I'm here to get you instead," Angie explained. "Here, let me help you with your gear." She opened the rear door of the van and reached for Debbie's pack.

Deb clutched her backpack a little tighter. "Why'd you have to change the plans? I wanted to go home with my friends."

"Please don't make a scene, Deb," Angie said in a hushed voice. "Just get in the van."

"What's wrong with me going home with Amelia and Paige? Huh?" She didn't care that her voice was rising or that her fellow Pathfinders were glancing over. But her mom very obviously did mind.

"We can discuss it in the van," Angie said through clenched teeth.

Mother and daughter glared at each other, until finally Debbie flung her backpack into the van and slammed herself into the passenger seat. She crossed her arms, scowling as her mother headed up the gravel drive to the road.

"I told you there was a change of plans," Angie began but Debbie interrupted her.

"What change of plans?" Angie didn't answer right away and Debbie sniffed, shaking her head. "That's what I thought."

"I told you we would discuss it in the van," her mom began slowly, "but you got angry so quickly you didn't even give me a chance to explain."

"You couldn't just say, 'Such and such is happening so I came to get you.' You have to make a big deal about it."

"I'm not comfortable talking about personal things in public, Deb. It would be nice if you could be a bit more accepting of who I am and what I'm comfortable with." She glanced at Debbie to see if she was listening. "Your grandmother fell last night and hurt her hip. She's in the hospital. Your dad is already there, and I picked you up so we could go see her as well."

"Is she okay?" Debbie's voice was a guilty whisper.

"She will be. Her hip is badly bruised, but the x-rays show it's not broken, thank goodness."

A few drops of rain splattered the windshield and Angie turned on the wipers. Debbie watched them squeak across the glass, her cheeks hot. She cracked her window open to get some fresh air.

"I'm sorry," she mumbled at last.

"Thank you."

Gradually the stuffy air inside the van was replaced by dampness as outside the rain fell harder. Debbie closed her window.

"Looks like we're going to get a good soaking," Angie commented, as if holding out a peace offering. "I'm glad it held off until now, though."

"It was real sunny on Saturday," Debbie said, accepting the forgiveness her mom was offering. "I didn't even need gloves when we went for our hike."

"Where'd you hike to, Whonnock Lake?"

"Yeah. It's real nice there. Maybe we could go this summer? I think you can even rent canoes there."

"Definitely we can go to Whonnock. I haven't been there for a long time. Come to think of it, I haven't been canoeing for years. Your dad and I used to go sometimes — just on Alouette River. One time we were paddling along and a river otter came and swam beside us."

"Really?" Debbie asked. "Cool." Her mom turned, smiling. Debbie grinned back.

"How did the menu work out?"

"Mostly good. Someone forgot to pack blueberries, so we had regular pancakes yesterday morning. But they were good. This morning Paige and Amelia and me had to make breakfast and we made the most amazing French toast. Everyone was begging for thirds!"

Angie laughed.

Debbie stared out the window, tracing a rivulet of water as it ran down the glass. She began to hum a song they'd learned the night before.

Lost in her thoughts, Debbie didn't notice right away that her mother had begun to sing the words. Slowly, realization crept over her and she turned.

"Mmhmm I want to linger,/ mmhmm a little longer,/ mmhmm a little longer here with you."

Debbie joined in, and they finished the song together. "Mmhmm it's such a perfect night,/ mmhmm it doesn't seem quite right,/ mmhmm that this should be my last with you."

For several seconds the car was silent except for the swish of the wipers.

"I always loved that song, even though it meant camp was over," Angie said at last.

"Yeah, some of the girls were crying," Debbie added. She didn't mention her own damp eyes.

"You have a lovely voice, Deb. I don't think I've ever heard you sing before."

Debbie blushed and picked uncomfortably at the cuff of her coat. "Oh, it's not that good."

Her mom put a hand on Debbie's knee. "When someone gives you a compliment, just say thank you," she suggested.

"Thank you. You have a nice voice too," Deb said.

"Thank you."

They looked at each other and laughed.

10 Playing Her Game

Debbie hovered in the narrow hallway outside the dressing rooms. Coach Steph stood talking to a parent, her back to Debbie. Was she ever going to finish and turn around? Debbie glanced at the clock, moving from foot to foot. She was running out of time, and she really wanted some time with Coach Steph.

Debbie's shoulders fell as her coach walked away down the hall, still talking with the parent. She smacked her stick against the cement wall and then headed back to the dressing room.

Coach Mitch looked up as Debbie came in and motioned her over.

"Where'd you go, Deb? I told all the wings we were going to meet before the game."

"Sorry, Coach, I had to ask my mom something," she mumbled, slumping down on the bench, her feet stuck out in front of her.

When warm-up was over, Debbie skated to the

bench and sat beside Hannah. She stared across the ice, hunting for her parents. The spectators sat in two sets of benches — the visiting team's fans to the left of the penalty boxes, the fans of the home team Hurricanes to the right. And right up at the wall, warmly dressed, hands wrapped around travel mugs filled with steaming lattes, were Debbie's mom and dad.

On the ice, the ref blew the whistle and Meghan's line skated into position. The puck dropped. With a flick of her wrist, Meghan drew the puck out of the face-off circle. Vanessa picked it up and skated into the Hurricanes end. Vanessa made a solid tape-to-tape pass back to Meghan. Deftly bypassing a line of green Hurricanes jerseys, Meghan skated close to the goal line. She shot the puck up off the goalie, over the net, over the glass, and into the stands. The whistle blew and play stopped.

"Charlie, Deb, Amelia, get out there," Coach Steph said.

Debbie skated to the right of the face-off circle and got into position. The Hurricanes won the face-off. Their winger skated through the neutral zone with the puck into the Lightning zone. Amelia intercepted and shot the puck down the ice. Debbie picked up the puck and fired a pass over to Charlie, who caught the pass and took off down the ice, Debbie and Amelia right behind her.

Charlie tossed a pass to Debbie, who skated toward

the blue line. Amelia got some speed, found some open ice, and tapped her stick on the ice. Debbie sent her the puck. Amelia caught it and skated hard for the net. Charlie was already in the slot, but the Hurricanes defence was closing in hard and fast. Amelia wound up, faked the shot, and passed instead. Charlie saw it coming and fired a one-timer at the net. It went top-shelf past the goalie and came to rest in the back of the yawning cage.

"YEAH! YEAH! YEAH!" Debbie and the rest of her line dog-piled Charlie as the players on the bench screamed.

Meghan's line skated out to centre ice. The Hurricanes centre won the draw and dished it toward the wing. The player carried the puck across centre ice and into the Lightning end. As the Lightning defence moved in on her, she made a drop pass behind her to the centre. Hannah checked the centre and managed to gain possession of the puck, but then she lost an edge and fell. The Hurricanes centre skated away.

"Come on, Lightning!" Debbie cried from the bench. She leaned forward so she could see over the boards, her whole body twisting and turning with the players on the ice.

The rest of the Lightning scrambled to fill the gap Hannah had left, but the centre reached the net and took the shot. Kira went down, trapping the puck in her gear.

The referee whistled down the play and they moved to the left of Kira for another face-off. This time Meghan won the draw and passed it to Vanessa. Vanessa headed toward centre ice with the puck.

"Head up, Vanessa!" Coach Steph cried from the bench.

Vanessa stumbled, but caught her balance just in time to move out of reach of a challenging Hurricanes defender. She looked around for someone to pass to, but no one was in position, so she skated around behind the net and waited, avoiding the oncoming defence.

Mentally Debbie was on the ice with Vanessa. She had the puck; she waited for Meghan and Hannah to get in position. What would she do? Who would she pass to? Where would she skate next?

"Get in there and support her, Meghan!" Coach Steph called. "Come on, girls!"

Meghan managed to shake off the opposition harassing her and skated up to the left of the goal. Vanessa passed her the puck, but the shot was too hard and Meghan had to skate after it. A Hurricanes winger picked it off. She reached centre ice unchecked as the Lightning players scrambled to catch her. At the Lightning blue line, she passed off, and in another second the Hurricanes had scored.

Still, at the second intermission the Lightning were up by two goals. The girls sat on the bench talking and joking with one another while the coaches planned behind them.

"We're on fire tonight!" Hannah said and squirted water into her mouth. It dribbled down her chin and soaked the front of her jersey.

"Did you see that shot? I don't think their goalie even knew it was coming!" Meghan said. "I think she was screened by her own defence!"

"We've got it now, that's for sure."

"We're making Swiss cheese out of that goalie!"

"Okay, girls, listen up," Coach Steph said. She outlined what she wanted them to do. "You're playing really well, let's keep it up. Stick to the game plan."

"Yeah, these Hurricanes are nothing but a big wind!" Vanessa shouted.

Appreciative laughter rose up around her, but Coach Mitch shot her a warning look. "Just get out there and play your game, girls," he said. "There's still one more period. Play smart and don't be overconfident."

Coach Steph cleared her throat. "Coach Mitch is right," she said. "When you start getting too sure of yourselves, that's when you get lazy, make mistakes, and lose your advantage."

Debbie leaned forward on the bench as Meghan's line skated out for the start of the third period, her coaches' words running through her head. She had to keep playing her game.

Debbie stretched her shoulders, leaning back until she bumped into something solid. A strong hand squeezed her shoulder and, glancing back, Debbie saw that it was Coach Steph. Debbie turned back to the ice. She felt good tonight — confident. She smiled to herself. Maybe hockey really was her game.

11 Stepping on Toes

"It's this next street," Debbie directed as Angie turned the corner. "That big house on the left."

Angie pulled into the driveway and turned off the ignition. "You've got everything? All your gear for tomorrow morning?"

"Yeah."

"Don't stay up all night — Coach Steph won't appreciate two tired players tomorrow morning," Angie warned as they hoisted Debbie's bags from the back of the van.

"Mom!"

"What? I'm your mother; I'm allowed to give advice. It's part of the job description."

Debbie reached out and rang the bell. From inside the house, Debbie heard the tap of shoes on tile, and then the front door opened.

"Deb, Angie, come on in," Coach Steph said, standing back. "Amelia, Deb is here," she called out.

"Hey, Deb. Hi, Mrs. Lowell," Amelia said, standing next to her mother. Coach Steph's arm slipped around her daughter's shoulders. Amelia leaned against her mother, watching as Debbie untied her shoes.

"Thanks for having Deb over," Angie said. She pulled her keys from her pocket and turned toward the door. "We'll have to have Amelia over to our place soon."

"Oh, it's no problem," Coach Steph replied with a smile. She dropped her arm and pulled the door open for Angie. "We're happy to have her. Amelia's got the whole evening planned out."

"Sounds like fun. Well, bye, Deb," Angie said. "I'll pick you up tomorrow morning after practice."

"Yeah, bye."

Her mom leaned over to hug her and Debbie awkwardly hugged her back, anxious for Angie to be gone. The door closed behind her and Debbie breathed a sigh of relief.

"Bring your stuff up to my room, Deb," Amelia told her, heading for the stairs. "We'll sleep up there tonight — it's more private. Aaron is always getting up and watching cartoons first thing Sunday morning. It's bad enough we have to get up early for practice. You definitely don't want Aaron waking you up even earlier than you have to!"

Debbie grabbed her pack and trailed behind Amelia up the stairs. At the curve, Debbie glanced down. Coach Steph had stopped at the table in the entry to pick some dead blooms from a flowering plant. "You really need some water, don't you?" she said. "We'll have to get you some, then." Whistling softly, she went into the kitchen.

"I got a bunch of magazines and tons of junk food. Deb?" Amelia called from the bedroom door. "Are you coming?"

"Yeah …"

They were sprawled across the lint-littered carpet reading and eating a half hour later, when there was a tap on the door.

"How's it going in here?" Coach Steph asked, poking her head in the room. "I'm going out to pick up a few things for supper."

Amelia looked up from her magazine and nodded. "Yeah, okay. Are you going to get the things on my list?"

"Are you paying?"

"Increase my allowance and maybe I could afford to."

"I'd love to increase your allowance. Too bad you never do anything to deserve a raise."

"I do more around here than you do, that's for sure. Always out at the beauty salon or getting your nails done."

Debbie looked from mother to daughter as they bantered back and forth. It seemed to come so easily to them. Was it because Amelia was Coach Steph's biological daughter? Debbie ached to join the conversation, to share just a little bit of what Amelia had, but she couldn't think of anything to say.

"See you in a bit. If you need anything, Dad's out in his workshop," Coach Steph told them and closed the door.

Amelia went back to reading her magazine, but Debbie couldn't focus on the player stats and articles. "You and your mom sure do get along well together."

"Most of the time, I guess."

"You have a lot in common," Debbie went on. "That probably helps."

Amelia sat up and crossed her legs. "We don't have that much in common. Just hockey, really."

"That's more than me and my mom." Debbie leaned over and took a handful of chips from the bowl between them. "We don't have anything in common. Her big thing right now is trying to find something we can do together."

"Really? What kinds of things has she found?"

"Well, we did this yoga class," Debbie said, shaking her head at the memory.

"Yoga? Cool. That's supposed to be really good for flexibility and stuff. Didn't you like it?" Amelia leaned back against her bed and hugged her knees to her chest.

"I was lousy at it," Debbie confessed. "But my mom did great. Like she'd been doing it forever."

"Kind of like me and my mom with hockey. She's this legend of the game, and I could hardly stay up on my skates when I started," Amelia said with a little laugh. Then she shrugged. "But I just kept trying."

"Well, I'm definitely not going back to yoga," Debbie said firmly.

Amelia grinned and stood up. "Come on, let's go kick my brother off the air hockey. I bet I can whip your butt at that!"

★ ★ ★

After supper Mr. Larsen and Aaron left for the movies and Debbie settled on the couch in the family room with Amelia and her mother to watch the movies Amelia had rented.

The girls sat on either side of Coach Steph, feet resting on the ottoman that served as a coffee table as well as a footrest. A very large bowl of heavily buttered popcorn sat nestled on Coach's lap. Debbie leaned back against the cushions as Amelia started the movie.

"What's this one?" Coach asked, helping herself to some popcorn.

Amelia grinned as she waved the empty case. "A romantic comedy we've been dying to see."

Debbie made a face. Romantic comedy? Surely Coach Steph wasn't interested in such girlie movies. But apparently she was, judging by the smile and nod.

"Perfect for girls' night, then. Right, Deb?" she asked.

Debbie smiled eagerly, but before the opening credits had finished she was already half asleep. The couch was very comfortable, the room was dusky, and if she tilted even a couple of inches to her left she'd brush Coach Steph's shoulder. Smiling for real this time, she closed her eyes.

"Deb?"

Debbie opened her eyes and blinked. Had she fallen asleep? She was leaning against Coach Steph, one arm draped across her body. She pulled her arm away and sat up. Amelia glared at her and Debbie flushed.

"Sorry," she muttered.

"That's okay," Coach Steph said easily, reaching for the remote. "Deb's obviously a bit tired. Maybe we shouldn't try for all three movies tonight." She pressed *play* and sat back against the cushions.

Voices filled the room and Debbie concentrated on the screen. After a while Amelia stopped glaring at her and turned to face the TV as well. All three watched the movie in silence.

12 Mothers

Debbie and Paige were among the first to arrive Wednesday evening for their Pathfinder meeting. Only Kelsie and Amelia were seated around a folding table set up in the middle of the room, their program books all over the scarred wooden surface. Kelsie looked up and waved hello as the two girls came in. Amelia studied her fingernails. Diana was at the stage, rummaging through her bin of materials.

"Hey, girls," she said over her shoulder. Paige waved as they both found chairs.

"Where is everyone else?" Debbie asked sitting down.

"Late, as usual," Kelsie said. "How hard is it to be on time for a meeting?"

"If you had my mother, you'd never be late for anything," Paige confided. "She's wound completely tight about it."

"My mom is the exact opposite," Kelsie said. She

pulled her long hair over her shoulder and began braiding it. "If she's supposed to be somewhere at seven, she leaves at seven." The other girls laughed. "It's true! It's embarrassing too. I stand at the door with all my stuff and my shoes on, and she'll say, 'Oh, I just need to touch up my makeup.' Or, 'I should really just clear these dishes.' Then, a half hour later, when I'm asleep ..." Another burst of laughter filled the room.

Kelsie snapped her gum and grinned. She tossed her braid over her shoulder and leaned her elbows on the table. "One time Mom decided to have a shower ten minutes before we had to leave for my sister's dance recital. You should've heard Kendra! Oh, my God!"

Diana dropped some papers on the table. "Kelsie Davis, you're exaggerating. I've known your mother for a long time, and she's not that bad."

"Come on, Diana," Kelsie said, stretching her arms across the table toward their leader. "You can't tell me my mom hasn't left you waiting somewhere."

Diana opened her mouth then closed it again and the girls screamed with laughter again. "Well, she's not as bad as you're making her out to be," Diana said.

"You should hear what Mia says about you," Kelsie teased. She leaned in to Debbie. "Last year, Diana's daughter Mia was in our unit. She had great stories about Diana. Too bad she's gone to the Rangers now."

"Never mind Mia's stories, Kels," Diana warned.

"Are we going to get on with our meeting tonight?"

"What are we supposed to be doing?" Debbie asked, reaching for the open calendar lying on the table.

"We're supposed to be working on program stuff," Diana began as the door opened and a couple more girls came in.

"Why are you guys late?" Paige asked. "Was it your mother's fault?"

The taller of the two girls snorted. "Everything is my mother's fault."

"Tell me about it," her friend agreed. "Right now it's my mother's fault I didn't make the senior cheer squad at my gym. 'Jada, you're overdoing it. You're going to hurt yourself'," she mimicked in a high nasally voice. "The girl who got on was practicing twice as much as me. I could have killed my mother! She always thinks she knows better! Just 'cause she used to coach gymnastics, she thinks she's got to coach me too."

"Well, she might know what she's talking about," Diana suggested.

"Whatever."

"You know," Diana said, "believe it or not, we mothers do sometimes know what we're talking about."

Loud objections filled the room. Diana raised a hand. When it was quiet again, she continued. "Despite what you think, we are always thinking of what is best for our kids. I always told Mia that my job was to keep her safe. That's still my job. That's your mom's job too, Jada. And yours, Kelsie, and Deb and Paige."

"My mom can't turn off her coach's switch," Amelia said. "All she thinks about is hockey and how I could play better. It's like it's the only thing she knows how to talk about. I don't even feel like I've got a mom half the time. It drives me crazy."

The other girls around the table cast sympathetic glances at Amelia, who was very busy digging holes in the table edge with her pencil. "Sometimes I think I should just quit hockey completely."

"At least your mother is interested in what you do!" Debbie cried. "My mom doesn't know anything about hockey or any other sports. All she's interested in is her stupid music. I'd love to have your mother, at least she gets you."

Debbie clamped her mouth shut, wishing she could un-say what had just come out of it. But understanding laughter met her.

"Everyone else's mother is always better," Jada agreed. "It's the mother you have to live with that's the problem. All my friends adore my mother. 'Oh, Jada, you have the coolest mom!' they're always gushing. 'Oh, Jada, I absolutely love your mom! I wish she were my mom! Maybe she could show me how to dress like that!' It drives me insane."

"Your mom is an amazing dresser, Jada," Kelsie said.

"Yeah, she is," Jada agreed.

"So what happened to you?" Paige asked, glancing at Jada's frayed jeans and black hoodie. Jada stuck out her tongue.

"The thing I liked best about my mom when I was a girl," Diana broke in, "was that she would get a bunch of my friends together and we'd spend all afternoon baking the most amazing things — fancy cookies, elaborate cakes, pastries. Then we'd eat them."

"My mom's a lousy cook," Paige said. "But she's real good at finding restaurants! And," she continued over the laughter, "she and I have a blast going to the theatre together. I'd rather do that than have a spotless house, I guess."

Several of the girls nodded but Debbie frowned, her emotions swirling inside like the clothes in the washing machine. She wasn't the only one who thought she had the wrong mother? But all the girls gathered around the table, including Amelia, who was still poking her pencil into the table, were with their biological mothers. And, obviously, they loved their mothers, despite their differences. Debbie closed her eyes, suddenly tired. It was all way too much to think about.

13 No Contact

"Deb, come in and set the table for dinner, please," Angie called out the door.

"I'll be in soon," Debbie promised. "I just want to practice shooting a bit more."

"You don't have time now. We have to eat and get you to your game."

"Yeah, yeah …"

The front door closed and Debbie was immediately lost in concentration.

When Angie appeared on the driveway five minutes later, her face was tight with anger. She snatched up the puck, grabbed Debbie's arm, and almost shoved her into the house.

"What is your problem?" Debbie cried, wrenching away from her mother's grip. "I was working on something important!"

"I asked you five minutes ago to come in and set the table," her mother said. "And you chose not to listen to me. Now dinner is getting cold and we're late. Clean up and get to the table."

They didn't say a word to each other all through dinner or on the drive to the rink. Debbie was still thinking about their fight once the game began and she wasn't jolted back into reality until she heard the crash of a couple players slamming into the boards. She looked around and decided it was a reality she could do without. Late in the third period, the Lightning trailed by a goal. It was a lousy game following a lousy day, and Debbie really wished it would hurry up and be over.

Across from the players' bench, parents and friends — including Angie — sat cheering both teams on. Why had her mother bothered to come? Why did she waste her time sitting around a cold ice rink watching a stupid game, when she could be playing her precious piano or doing yoga perfectly?

The whistle blew and Debbie and her linemates skated onto the ice. They took up their positions for the face-off. Amelia took the draw and swept it back for Debbie. Debbie skated along the boards, but the Sentinels wing was immediately all over her. Hannah skated in and, after a short skirmish, came up with the puck. She backhanded a pass to Amelia. Debbie skated behind the Lightning net. She picked up Amelia's pass but was poke-checked. Hannah skated hard to the loose puck, but the Sentinels wing beat her to it.

Debbie charged in for support and there was another scramble as the two teams fought for possession.

The Sentinels centre finally won it. She skated a few strides before passing off to her wing. The wing missed the pass. Debbie picked it up. Play quickly turned over as Hannah headed back across the centre line. Amelia got some speed and found open ice. "I'm open!" she screamed.

Debbie looked up and found her teammate. She sent the puck flying up-ice. But instead of aiming her pass to where Amelia was headed, Debbie sent the puck flying to where Amelia actually was. Amelia came to a screaming halt. She reached for the puck behind her, but a Sentinels wing was there. Debbie raced up the ice. She used her stick to knock the puck loose. Her stick tangled in the Sentinels wing's skate, and the girl went down.

The whistle blew and the ref's arm shot into the air. Penalty — Lightning.

"What?" Debbie cried. "Oh, come on, you've got to be kidding. That was a dive! She faked it!"

"That's your second penalty tonight. If you complain again," the ref warned, "I'll give you another penalty for unsportsmanlike conduct."

On the ice the play kept on getting away from the Lightning. Every time a Lightning player got possession, there seemed to be three Sentinels on top of her. Debbie watched from her penalty-box prison, feeling her frustration and anger rising with each missed pass, each missed opportunity to score.

The time was winding down on Debbie's penalty when the play moved in front of the box. Meghan and an opponent battled for the puck, their sticks smacking the ice and the boards, their breath coming in short, hard puffs.

"Get it, Meghan!" Debbie cried, standing. "Come on! Get in there and help her out, Vanessa!"

Vanessa skated in, but the Sentinels player was taller and stronger. She outmaneuvered the two Lightning players and came up with the puck. In the skirmish, she tripped Meghan. Debbie looked to the ref for the whistle, but none came.

"Come on, Ref! Call it both ways!" Debbie yelled.

Meghan got up and skated after the play as the door to the penalty box opened and Debbie skated out. Coach Mitch signalled Debbie off the ice, and she headed toward the bench. But then the player who had tripped Meghan skated past. Without thinking, Debbie stuck out her stick, caught the player's foot, and sent her to the ice. The whistle blew then, long and hard.

★ ★ ★

Debbie was alone in the dressing room, slumped against the wall. Her teammates had all dressed and left quicker than they'd ever done before, with almost no post-game chat. A few had shot her sympathetic glances but mostly they'd avoided looking at her.

"What was that all about, Deb?"

Debbie couldn't meet her coach's eyes. Under normal circumstances Debbie would have been thrilled to have Coach Steph's undivided attention. But not like this.

"What were you thinking? Were you even thinking?"

Debbie turned her head ever so slightly, caught a glimpse of Coach Steph's angry face, and shifted her glance away again. "I don't know," she muttered.

"Pardon?"

"I said, I don't know." She jabbed the heel of her shoe into the rubber floor.

"I want more of an answer than that."

"I was mad because that other player tripped Meghan and the stupid ref didn't call it," Debbie finally blurted out. "He called me for everything tonight, but the other team could just do whatever they wanted!"

Coach Steph sat beside Debbie on the bench. "You have no control over what the referees do or don't do," she said. "What you do have control over are your own actions. I didn't see a lot of that tonight. Your penalty cost us a goal, Deb. And besides all that, you didn't follow coach's directions when Coach Mitch called you over to the bench, did you?"

"It wasn't like we were winning or anything."

Debbie felt Coach Steph stiffen beside her and

remorse flooded through her. "Sorry," she muttered. "You're right, I cost us a goal. Are you going to bench me?"

"Yes," Coach said. "You're one member of this team, Deb. Each member has her own job to do to help the whole team do well. Tonight you didn't do your job and the team paid the price."

Debbie's shoulders sunk under the weight of her coach's disappointment. She longed for Coach Steph to be angry with her. At least with anger, she could be angry right back.

"Go home now. We'll see you at practice." Coach Steph left the room.

When Debbie emerged from the dressing room a few minutes later, her mom was waiting in the hall. Angie didn't say anything as they walked out of the building, but Debbie could see the disappointment and sorrow in her eyes. Debbie kept her eyes to the ground. Neither of them said a word as they loaded the bag into the back of the van and climbed in. Debbie leaned her head against the seat, closed her eyes, and waited. And waited. And waited.

They were almost home and still Angie had said nothing about the game. Nothing about Debbie's stupid penalties, about how disappointed Angie was in her, how embarrassing it was to have your daughter spending most of the game in the penalty box. Nothing. Not a word.

Was it going to be a big explosion once they got home? Debbie wished she would just get it over with. Just like with Coach Steph, Debbie wanted Angie to be angry, to just blast her. Then Debbie could blast back and they could be done with it.

Angie pulled into the tidy garage. She turned off the engine, pulled the keys from the ignition, and started to climb out of the van.

"Aren't you going to yell or anything?" Debbie demanded. She felt as though she were suffocating.

"No," her mom said, pulling her feet back into the car. "I figured you would talk to me when you were ready."

Debbie frowned. Usually the adults in Debbie's life had plenty to say when Debbie screwed up, and didn't hesitate to say it. "You're not going to give me a lecture, or tell me how I let the team down, how disappointed you are, like Coach Steph?"

"I'm your mother. It's not my job to coach you."

Debbie looked down at her hands. She noticed a hang nail and picked at it until it stung and burned. She stuck her finger in her mouth. The silence was growing, filling the space in the van like air fills a balloon. She needed to escape.

But Debbie didn't move. Why didn't she just open the van door and climb out? There were good TV shows on, and there was a new online game Amelia had told her about that she wanted to try. Heck, there was even unfinished homework. So why didn't Debbie get out?

"The refereeing tonight was pathetic," she heard herself saying. "He called me on everything and let the other team get away with tons of stuff!"

"I imagine it would be very frustrating to think you're being unfairly penalized," Angie said. "But is that what was really bothering you out there?"

Debbie pressed her picked finger, glad of the sting. She concentrated on that sting, pressing harder when it subsided. "No."

"I found it really hard to concentrate on the game tonight, myself. I was angry and frustrated because you hadn't done as I'd asked you, when I'd asked you."

Maybe Debbie should have gotten out of the car when she'd had a chance. Now her mother would expect her to apologize. Debbie stiffened as Angie began to speak again.

"But every time you went in the penalty box I felt guilty because I realized I had made you angry and frustrated too, and so neither of us was concentrating on the game. I could have dealt with the situation in a better way and I'm sorry."

Debbie looked up, startled by the unexpected apology. "You're sorry?"

Her mom nodded. Debbie struggled with the emotions going through her. No adult had ever apologized to her before. It had always been Debbie's job to say she was sorry. Angie was looking at her, a small hopeful smile on her face. A strange urge crept through Debbie.

"I'm sorry too," she heard herself saying. "I should've come in when you asked me to. I was just really into what I was doing."

"Yes, I should have seen that. I can't stand it when your dad tries to drag me away from the piano when I'm working on something."

Angie squeezed Debbie's arm. Debbie could feel the warmth through the fabric of her sweater, even after her mother dropped her hand.

"No one's ever said they were sorry to me before," Debbie whispered.

"No, I imagine they didn't, Deb." Debbie felt her mother's hand smoothing her hair. "But they will now."

Tears stung Debbie's eyes and she cleared her throat, brushing a hand across her face. She felt a strange feeling, sort of like the first time she was in a swimming pool. Even though she didn't know how to swim, the water supported her, allowed her to float. It was the most amazing sensation.

"Relationships are tricky things," her mom continued a few seconds later. "They require a lot of work, all the time. You have to be willing to talk about things, listen to the other person, and, most of all, apologize when you're wrong. But it's worth the work."

"No one ever cared about my side before," Debbie

confessed. "They never listened. Well, maybe my social worker, but she was the only one."

Angie smiled at Debbie and ruffled her hair. "You can talk to me about anything, sweetie. I will always care about your side of things. Always."

14 Not Our Thing

"I've got an extra rehearsal tonight for our concert," Angie announced as the family sat down to dinner Thursday evening. "So you guys will be on your own. Think you can handle it?"

"See ya," Greg said with a wave of his fork.

"Paige is coming over after dinner," Debbie told her parents. "We're going to work on a thing for social studies. Is that okay?" She looked from one parent to the other.

"Absolutely," Angie said. "We haven't seen much of Paige lately."

"Huh." Debbie studied the food on her plate. Paige had said the same thing. Debbie was hoping that agreeing to be her partner for this Ancient Greece project would smooth things over a bit.

"Did Paige give you that course schedule today?" Angie asked. "Her mom said she'd send it to school with her."

"Yeah, it's in my bag somewhere." Debbie speared a piece of potato and ate it. "You taking a class or something?"

"Well actually," Angie began, "I was hoping we might take a class …"

Debbie's head shot up, already shaking "no way." But Angie held up a hand.

"Hear me out, okay?" Reluctantly Debbie nodded. "Thank you. There's a class at Scrapper's Haven this weekend for moms and daughters. I thought we could take it with Paige and her mom."

Debbie swallowed a groan. Scrapbooking? Debbie was not an arts and crafts kind of person; surely her mother had figured that out by now. But her mother was looking at her so hopefully Debbie realized she hadn't.

"I'm not really into ribbons and flowery paper," she hedged.

"Really?" Angie teased. "I'd never have guessed. I'm not either, Deb. But this class is to make a small memory book. We'll take our own photographs and then put them together so they represent who we are. I thought it sounded like a neat project for us."

"What kind of photos?" Debbie asked.

It wasn't like there were tons of pictures of her. She didn't have any from when she was a baby, or even a little kid. She had a few pictures taken when she lived with her foster family, but it was a pretty pathetic collection.

Darlene and Steve were always more interested in taking pictures of their own kids, Nadine and Jason. Half the time, Debbie had been the one taking the pictures so the "whole family" could be in the shot. A wave of bitterness swelled in Debbie's gut. She swallowed hard.

"Whatever kinds of photos you want," her mom said. "Some people might do baby pictures, but that doesn't mean you have to. I know we can get a good collection from the past year."

Debbie laughed and felt the bitterness fade away. Someone was always taking a picture of her since she'd moved in with the Lowells, especially Gran and Pops. The most recent pictures were of Gran demonstrating her skill with the cane she now had to walk with. But still. Poker nudged her thigh and Debbie slipped a piece of zucchini to him, giggling when he spat it out and left it lying on the kitchen floor. She scratched his ears and a thought began to form.

"I could do something with me and Poker," she said.

"Perfect," her mom said with a smile. "Why don't you let Paige know we'll join them?"

★ ★ ★

A large table was set up at the back of the stationery store when they arrived the following Saturday afternoon. It had been covered with brown paper, and at each chair was a pile of paper, some glue, and scissors. In the middle of the table was even more stuff. Debbie

115

took a chair beside Paige and Angie slid into the chair on her other side.

"You remembered the photos, right?" she whispered to her mother.

"Yes, Deb, you asked me that before we left home. I've got them right here." Angie held up the envelope.

When the seats were filled the instructor introduced herself. "Welcome everyone. This afternoon we're going to create a small keepsake book. I hope you've all brought some pictures to use? Great. Let's get started."

Some of the people in the class had obviously done this scrapbooking stuff before, Debbie guessed, judging by how quickly they finished each step, and how beautiful their pages looked when they were completed. Even Paige and her mom were moving right along. Debbie watched as the teacher demonstrated the different techniques, but when she tried to do it herself, her pages never came out quite the way she had planned.

The only good thing was that her mom was having just as much trouble. "Deb," Angie whispered, "did you see how to do that thing with the chalk?"

"Sort of," Deb whispered back. She held up her own square of paper and showed her mother what she'd done. "You kind of brush it across the edge of the paper like this." She brushed her cotton ball across the edges of the paper, but there was too much chalk on the cotton and a big splotch of colour stained the page. Debbie snorted, then quickly covered her mouth.

"I'm glad it's not just me," her mom confessed.

Everyone else had finished and was waiting when Debbie and Angie finally finished their chalked pages. Debbie looked around the table, her face heating up. Were they that slow?

"Everyone ready?" the instructor asked, glancing around the table. "Good. Now, find your pieces of chipboard and the blue patterned paper," she said, holding up a curly bit of brown cardboard and a piece of paper. "This is a very effective way to add embellishment to your pages," she said when everyone had their materials in hand. She went on to demonstrate how to achieve "a nice weathered look."

Next time Mom wants to try some mother/daughter thing, Debbie thought as she spread glue over one side of her chipboard, *I'm going to insist on full-contact football*.

She got the patterned paper stuck down and pounded it to the chipboard with the side of her fist. Paige raised her eyebrows. "What are you doing?" she whispered.

"Making sure it's well stuck."

"I think it's well stuck," Paige said with a grin. Debbie stuck out her tongue. Then she found her craft knife and prepared to cut the beautiful curlicue.

"Ah, darn it!" she muttered as the knife slipped, slicing into the chipboard. Two knife slips later she was ready to sand. By then everyone else had moved to a second curlicue. Debbie glanced over at her mother. Angie's shoulders were hunched up around her ears and her lips had disappeared in a tight, thin line.

Somehow they managed to get to the end of the class and the last page of their mini-books. As everyone was clearing up the scraps, the teacher handed out coupons for free merchandise. Angie and Debbie looked at their coupons and started laughing. Paige and her mom frowned, confused.

"What's so funny, you guys?" Paige asked.

"Nothing," Debbie sputtered. "But you can have my coupon." She handed the slip of paper to her friend.

Angie handed hers to Paige's mom. "Yes, you two go ahead and use ours."

They gathered up their books and headed out to the car. Debbie thumbed through her book as Angie made her way out of the parking lot. One photo had been cropped too much and part of Poker's left ear was missing. On one page she had smudged the ink, and on another she had gotten a little overenthusiastic with the glue. She smiled and touched the last photo in the book — one of her, Poker, and her new mom and dad, taken on their family camping trip the summer before.

"You know what?" Debbie asked.

"What?"

"That was fun."

"It was fun," Angie agreed. She glanced at Debbie and smiled. "Even if we weren't very good at it."

"No," Debbie agreed. "Scrapbooking is definitely not our thing."

15 Fighting for Possession

Greg dropped Debbie off for practice early Sunday morning with an encouraging smile. He reached across the car and squeezed her arm. "It'll be okay, Deb."

Dragging her equipment bag behind her, Debbie went up the stairs of the ice centre. What kind of reception would she get from her teammates? Was everyone really pissed off at her? They certainly had a right to be. She was tempted to just hide out in the lobby until her dad came back to get her.

Debbie opened the heavy door and maneuvered her bag through. Hannah and one of the other wings were the only ones left in the dressing room. They looked up as Debbie came in and nodded silently. Debbie sat down and bent over to unzip her bag. Right on top, tucked into her glove, was a piece of paper. Curious, she leaned over and picked it up.

"Hi, Deb," it said, in her mother's handwriting. "Have a really good practice. Put the last game out of your head and look forward to your next one. Dad and I are proud of you and we love you. Mom."

Debbie bent over her bag to hide her embarrassment and confusion. Why had her mom done that? No one had ever sent Debbie a note or a letter before. Especially one like that. She paused from taping her socks and picked up the note. As she read the words again a strange little current of happiness spread through her. As the two girls approached, heading for the door, Debbie thrust the note in the waistband of her hockey pants. The girls grabbed their sticks and left Debbie alone in the dressing room.

"Anyone left in here?" Coach Steph called out, pushing open the door.

"Deb, you made it. Let's get a move on though. It's seven."

Debbie looked down at her skates and groaned. "Coach Steph?" Debbie's pulse quickened and her mouth felt dry. She did not like apologizing. Her coach paused and turned back. Debbie cleared her throat. "I just wanted to, you know, apologize for the other day. You know, at the game."

"I appreciate your apology, Deb," Coach Steph said. "But you should apologize to your teammates. Your penalties affected them more than me."

Debbie said nothing.

"Come on, the team is waiting for us," Coach Steph said, finally.

Still Debbie couldn't bring herself to move. Coach turned again. "It's always best to just get unpleasant things over with, Deb," she said. She reached for Debbie's hand, but Debbie threw her arms around her coach and held on. For a second Coach Steph hugged her back, then she patted Debbie firmly on the shoulder and stepped away.

The girls were in the middle of a drill when Debbie joined them on the ice, but Coach Steph called them over to the bench. When they were all gathered she nodded at Debbie.

Debbie took a deep breath, trying not to make eye contact with anyone. "I just wanted to say I'm sorry for what happened at our game the other day," she blurted out. "I was mad and I didn't think about the team. So, I hope you'll forgive me." She looked up then, head tilted to one side, hoping to find some friendly faces. Most of the girls smiled or nodded, but Meghan stepped forward and cleared her throat.

"Thanks, Deb," she said. "And I just wanted you to know that I appreciated you standing up for me."

"Really?"

"Yeah. Even though you got a penalty for it and we lost the game." Meghan grinned and several of the girls laughed. "You can be our goon."

Even the coaches laughed at that. Debbie grinned and ducked her head as Meghan swatted her shoulder.

For the last fifteen minutes of the practice, Coach

Steph split the team into two groups and got them playing a mini-game. Debbie started at right wing, Meghan at centre, and Hannah at left wing. Across the centre line from Debbie was Amelia. She hadn't spoken a word to Debbie the entire time they'd been on the ice.

Meghan won the face-off and snapped the puck to Debbie. Debbie picked up the pass and skated forward. Amelia was right there, challenging hard.

"That's it, Amelia," Coach called out, "press her. Use your stick. Deb, don't let her get it away from you! Use body position to protect the puck. Come on, put some strength into it. Pressure! Pressure!"

Amelia finally gained possession and skated away. Debbie turned and skated after her. Amelia sent the puck on a cross-ice pass to Vanessa. Vanessa picked it up and carried it in deep. Hannah moved forward, challenging her. Vanessa swerved to one side to avoid a collision and lost control of the puck. Debbie was right there. She snagged the puck, turned, and skated back across the blue line. She could feel someone behind her, could hear her breathing, and she skated harder. She crossed the centre line, sidestepped the other side's defence and crossed the blue line.

"Take the shot, Deb!" Coach Steph yelled.

Debbie fired a wrist shot on goal, and it ricocheted off Kira's goal stick. Meghan was right there and picked up the rebound as Debbie skated in to the far side of the net. Meghan fired from a bad angle and the shot went wide. Debbie and Amelia battled along the boards for possession. This time Debbie came up with it. She skated around behind the net and came out on the far side. Her shot went in on the short side.

Debbie pumped her arms in the air, a huge smile plastered across her face. Meghan and Hannah smacked her on the back.

"Good job, Deb!" Coach Steph said, skating in.

Debbie threw her arms around her coach and hugged her for the second time that morning. Suddenly she felt herself being wrenched away. Spinning around unsteadily, she came face to face with an angry Amelia.

"Hey, hey," Coach Steph said, stepping between Debbie and her daughter. "What's the deal, Amelia?"

Amelia's face was damp with sweat and tears. "You've got your own mother, Debbie," she said in a low, mean voice. "Get away from mine."

"I don't know what you're talking about," Debbie mumbled.

As Coach Mitch took over the practice, Coach Steph led Amelia and Debbie off the ice and onto the bleachers.

"Do you think I'm stupid?" Amelia asked. "Maybe I am, actually. I thought you wanted to be my friend."

Debbie opened her mouth to argue, but what could she say? She closed it again.

"Girls, what exactly is this about?" Coach Steph asked, looking from one to the other.

"Why don't you explain, Deb?" Amelia suggested. "Why don't you tell my mother all about your little scheme to become friends with me just so you could cozy up to her? Go on! Tell her!"

"Amelia, sweetie, calm down," Coach Steph said, putting a hand on her daughter's arm. Amelia wrenched away. She turned to Debbie and waited.

"It's not the way she's making it sound," Debbie began.

"Then how is it?" Amelia's anger filled the space between them, leaving Debbie speechless. She wasn't even sure, anymore, what she'd wanted or been trying to do.

"I did want to be friends with you, Amelia," Debbie began. "I —"

"I should have known there was something weird," Amelia broke in. "You wanting to practice with me all of a sudden and always coming to my house. How come we couldn't ever do stuff at your house? Huh?"

"We could do stuff at my house," Debbie said. "It was just that my mom teaches …"

"Whatever, Deb," Amelia broke in. "Whatever lies you have to tell yourself."

"Hey, Amelia," her mother cautioned.

"What, Mom? It's true! All Deb wanted was to spend time with you! She used me."

"I didn't use you. I didn't! We have a lot in common …"

"You have a lot in common with my mom, you mean," Amelia snarled. "You never wanted to be friends with me. You just wanted to get close to my mom. You even said at Pathfinders that you wish she was your mother!"

"And so what if I do?" Debbie demanded. "At least I appreciate your mom! You don't know how good you've got it! You said you should just quit hockey, you were so tired of your mom coaching you all the time!"

Amelia's face went white and her bottom lip trembled. She jumped to her feet, her eyes flashing. "Stay away from my mother, Deb Lowell. You've got your own mother." She pinned Debbie with her glare for one long second, then she stormed away.

Debbie stared hard at her feet waiting to be yelled at. But there was only quiet breathing. Finally Debbie looked up to find Coach Steph watching her.

"My mom and I don't have much in common," Deb said. "But I do with you."

"You're right," Coach Steph said with a smile, "we do share a love of hockey and sport. And that's great. I enjoy the time we spend together on the ice. But I'm not your mother, Deb. I'm your coach."

Debbie felt terrible. Tears burned her eyes and she squeezed them tightly shut. She would not cry. Coach Steph stood up. Debbie looked up through her helmet's cage. There, behind her coach, was her mom.

Guilt and embarrassment flooded Debbie as she realized her mom had heard her conversation with Coach Steph, and likely Amelia's accusations too. She turned away, sure her mom hated her now.

Her mom and the coach spoke in low voices. Then she heard Coach Steph leave.

Angie sat next to Debbie on the bench. After a few minutes of silence she turned Debbie to face her. At first Debbie resisted, but her mom persisted. Angie reached over, undid the strap of Debbie's helmet, and lifted it off her head. She smoothed back the loose brown hairs and cupped Debbie's chin with her hand. She leaned her head in until she was touching foreheads with Debbie.

"You felt a really strong connection with Coach Steph," she whispered.

Debbie nodded against her mom's head, her face suddenly wet. She wiped the tears away, but somehow they just kept coming.

"You're lucky to have such a good coach," Angie went on. "Coach Steph is very passionate about hockey, and she fills her players with that same enthusiasm. We have that in common, you and I, having something in our lives we're passionate about. Lots of people don't have anything at all."

"It's the only thing then," Debbie muttered, pulling away.

Her mom looked out across the empty stretch of ice. Slowly the ice cleaner went around and around, smoothing out the bumps and cuts, preparing for the next team.

"Relationships are about more than what you have in common," Angie said after a while. "Respecting each other, caring about each other, thinking the same way about things, those are important too. I don't share your love of basketball or hockey, that's true. And playing the piano isn't your thing. But we both like music. We love animals. We both like dumb sit-coms on TV."

"But I want my mom to like what I like! You just look at me like I'm speaking a whole different language when I talk about hockey or basketball …"

Angie's mouth tightened for a second. "This relationship thing goes two ways, Deb. You expect me to like sports and to be able to talk with you about them, but you haven't taken any effort to learn about my passions."

"I don't want to take piano lessons."

"I don't expect you to! Just like I don't want to learn how to ice skate. But I come to the rink and watch your practices and games. I cheer you on and encourage you. I make an effort."

Debbie squirmed. What her mother had said was true. She looked up at Angie, a bit sheepishly. Her mom reached for Debbie's hand.

"Relationships are hard work, Deb," she said.

"Remember what I said in the van the other day? We'll always have to work at it. We need to cut ourselves some slack because we've only been mother and daughter for a little over a year. Everyone else has a bit of a head start on us."

Debbie smiled, and suddenly realized she was feeling lighter than she had in a while.

16 The Right Note

"Nervous?" Debbie asked, leaning back on her mom's bed.

Angie stood sideways in front of the full-length mirror and looked critically at herself. "Nervous? Not really. Well, not about my playing, anyway. Maybe a bit nervous that everything goes smoothly … Does this skirt look too short?"

Debbie shook her head. "It looks fine. Besides, who's going to be looking at your feet?"

Angie tossed a rolled-up sock at Debbie. It missed her and landed on the floor. "Sock fights are for camp, Mom. And it's really not polite to throw things."

"You are much too saucy, young lady."

Debbie smiled as she watched her mom putter around the room, muttering to herself. Angie had been to the hairdresser that day and her short blond hair was carefully styled and sprayed. With her long black skirt and frilly white blouse, her makeup carefully applied,

Debbie hardly recognized her.

Greg came into the room whistling. "Are my girls ready yet? We need to get going, Ange."

"Yes, I'm almost — oh where is that necklace!" Angie cried.

Debbie slid off the bed and went to her mother's side. "Around your neck, Mom," she said.

Angie sagged a bit. "I guess I am a little nervous."

"Ya think?" Debbie said, smiling at her mother's reflection in the mirror.

"Go on, get out of here." Angie swatted Debbie's backside, but at least she was laughing.

At the theatre, Angie disappeared backstage to find her fellow performers while Greg and Debbie made their way to their seats. They found them right in the middle, halfway up. Paige and her mom were already there.

"Best place to be to launch popcorn at her while she's playing," Greg told Debbie.

"She'll kill you," Debbie warned him.

"She'll never know who it was."

Debbie shook her head and headed back out to the lobby. They'd arrived early enough that there was time to get a hot chocolate before the concert started. She could watch for Gran and Pops too. She peered through the crowds of people filing through the doors.

Finally, Debbie saw her grandparents push through the doors. She watched them slowly cross the crowded lobby, Gran leaning heavily on her cane and holding onto Pops' arm. Gran's hip was much better, but she was still unsteady.

"Deb, darling," Gran said, wrapping Debbie in a warm hug. She kissed her cheek, and then wiped the lipstick away with a soft tsk-tsk sound. "I always do that, don't I?" she whispered.

"That's okay," Debbie whispered in reply. "Hi, Pops. You look really handsome tonight."

"Thank you, thank you," he said, puffing out his chest. "You look pretty handsome yourself."

"Michael!" Gran said, shaking head at him. "You look lovely, Deb. Just lovely. Where are your parents, dear? Shouldn't we be getting inside?"

"Dad is waiting for you with Paige and her mom. Mom's backstage trying to convince herself she's not nervous."

Pops chuckled. "Angela always has nerves before she performs. But you watch, Deb," he said, his eyes shining with pride. "She'll forget there's an audience when she gets on stage."

"Come on, Father," Gran said, taking her husband's arm again. "This old girl needs to find her seat. Are you coming, Deb, dear?"

"I'll be there in a second. I want to finish my drink."

Debbie swallowed the last of her hot chocolate and dropped her empty cup into a garbage can. Next to it was a display rack for community events, groups, and services. She glanced at the brochures for service clubs, preschool programs, and art classes. She almost missed the narrow brochure hiding in the lower rack, but her eyes were pulled back by one word. She pulled the pamphlet from the rack.

"Hey, Deb, there you are!" Paige cried, rushing back to get Debbie. "They're telling us to take our seats."

"I'm coming!" Debbie tucked the pamphlet into her purse and followed after her friend.

They settled into their seats as the lights dimmed, and watched as Angie and the rest of the ensemble filed out onto the stage. Debbie kept her eyes on her mother as she sat down at the piano. Once the musicians had made sure their instruments were tuned, Angie played the opening chords of the concerto.

Debbie smiled as the familiar music filled the theatre. She'd been making an effort to listen when her mom practiced, and had even listened to a recording of this particular concerto played by an orchestra. For the first time, she saw how Angie lost herself in her playing. She noticed how Angie played with her whole body, not just her hands, feeling the music the way Debbie felt the ice beneath her feet, and felt the rough rubber of the basketball beneath her fingers. Something in common, she thought with a small grin.

At the end of the performance the audience was on its feet applauding. Greg whistled and Debbie yelled, clapping so hard her hands stung. The performers made their way off the stage and the applause died down as people left the theatre. Out in the lobby, Greg and Debbie pushed their way through the crowds to Angie.

"You were amazing, Mom." Debbie's voice was muffled by her mother's embrace. "I was so proud you were my mom."

"Thanks, Deb," Angie whispered against Debbie's hair. "You have no idea what that means to me."

★ ★ ★

"Are you sure you know where we're going?" Angie asked as she steered the van around a corner.

"Yes! I've got the directions right here. Don't you trust me?" Debbie asked.

"Well, yes, I do. But …"

"Then be quiet and take this right. There it is — the church on the left," Debbie told her, pointing. An old church building loomed in the dark March night. Angie pulled into the drive and found a place to park.

Angie slipped her purse over her shoulder, locked the car, and followed Debbie toward a brightly lit building just behind the church. "What is this? Are we going to a church service?"

"You'll see. Come on." Debbie grabbed her mom's hand.

Inside the door, Debbie stopped. She ran her damp hands down her jeans and took a breath.

"Good evening," a woman said, approaching them. "Can I help you?"

"I'm looking for Marta Svenson," Debbie said.

"I'm Marta."

"I'm Deb Lowell. I spoke to you on the phone the other day."

"It's a pleasure to meet you, Deb," Marta said, shaking Debbie's hand. "And this is your mother?"

"Yes, this is my mom, Angie."

"Welcome, welcome. We're always looking for new voices," Marta said, extending her hand to Angie.

Suddenly a bell sounded and people began moving toward a door at the back of the room.

"Oh, Stephen is ready to start — let's get in and we'll find you places to stand."

Marta led Debbie and her mom through a door into a large room. A piano stood in one corner, and fanned out in front of it were rows of chairs. Just about every chair was filled with chatting adults and kids.

Debbie turned to her mother, a big grin on her face. "This is the Maple Ridge Community Choir," she explained. "I thought it was something we could do — together."